Dirty London

Kelley York

This book is a work of fiction. Names, characters, places, and incidents are the product of the author's imagination or are used fictitiously. Any resemblance to actual events, locales, or persons, living or dead, is coincidental.

Visit her website at www.kelley-york.com.

Edited by Kelley York, Cover design by X-Potion Designs

ISBN-13: 978-1505701159 / ISBN-10: 1505701155

Manufactured in the United States of America
First Edition December 2014
The author acknowledges the copyrighted or trademarked status and trademark owners of the following wordmarks mentioned in this work of fiction: Hello Kitty, Fruit Loops, Rocky Horror Picture Show, Bubba Gump Shrimp, Alcatraz, Rainbow Brite, TV Guide

Other books by Kelley York

Hushed
Suicide Watch
Made of Stars

1

Diary of a Noble

I'd be an optimist if people didn't suck so much. As it is, with the general amount of suckage from most people I know, I consider myself a realist. I can be sad when bad things happen but I understand they will get better. I can be happy when good things happen but I'm smart enough to know that all good things eventually come to an end. Our suffering, our happiness, is never eternal. I see things for what they are. Bad shit happens to good people and vice-versa.

Some days are harder than others. I sit among my peers fully aware that I'm different. I'm aware that if they knew who I really am, it would be the end of my high school life. This, my dear diary, is the cost of going to a stuffy and severely conservative school. They don't accept different very well.

But I refuse to think there's anything wrong with me. I am normal. I am a human being just as deserving of love and happiness as the next person.

No, I am not the problem.

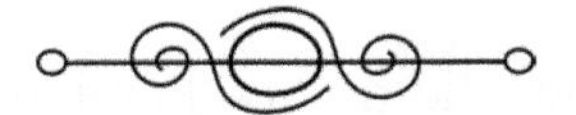

It's a smothering sort of day. Though the weather is cooling down for fall my uniform is itchy and stiff, and I'm restless listening to an awkward sixty-something teacher lecture us on the prolonged effects of the Korean War. I had lost my pen, to top it off, and the day's silver lining was when Mara Nitesh, seated in the desk beside mine, leaned over to offer me one of hers. God bless alphabetical seating. She didn't say anything but she *smiled*, and that's totally enough for me.

Honestly, most wouldn't think too much of Mara. I mean, if you saw her on the street you wouldn't stop her to ask if she's considered a career in modeling. She's not *that* kind of pretty. However she has these huge, almond-shaped eyes and the cutest way of chewing on her bottom lip when she's spacing off. Like she's doing right now. I'm trying to listen to Mrs. Scheck. I really am. How can I when I have that adorable face to stare at for an hour and a half?

The bell rings. Mara catches my eyes briefly as she stands and scoops her things into her backpack in one fluid motion. She graces me with another smile, pushes her long, dark hair over one shoulder...and then she's gone. I forgot to give the pen back.

I collect my things slowly, wanting to avoid the mob in the halls scrambling like rabbits to get out of school for the afternoon. Mara is still out there. I clutch her pen in my hand with every intention of marching up and giving it back to her. She's milling around with Trevor (her boyfriend) and his best friend Wade.

It's just a pen. No big deal. I'm not asking her to marry me.

Trevor spots me first and gives Mara a nudge so that she turns and cocks her head. "Hi, London."

You would think this is the first time I've ever talked to her. I mean, we've never had an interesting or in-depth conversation but we've exchanged words occasionally. I can't think of something witty or amusing to say, so instead I just offer out the Hello Kitty pen.

"You, uh, let me borrow this."

She starts to reach for it out of reflex, then pauses. "Oh! That's okay. You can keep it. I have a whole bag of them at home."

I lower my hand, sliding my thumb over the cap of the pen, feeling like an idiot standing there with Mara and the two boys staring at me like they're waiting for me to say something further. My mouth manages a smile. "Cool. Thanks."

As I'm turning to walk away I can hear them whispering amongst themselves, and then Trevor is calling, "Hey!" When I stop to look over my shoulder, he flashes me a grin. "You used to be in drama, right?"

I'm surprised he remembers eighth grade. Trevor and Wade I've known since middle school. Mara is a newer addition; she didn't move to town until freshman year of high school. Just because I knew Trevor doesn't mean he's ever paid any attention to me, much less the classes I've taken. "Yeah. Why?"

"We could use a new face at drama club," Mara says. "Mr. Cobb divided us up and each group is doing their own play, but we're a person short."

"And you want me to join?"

Trevor shrugs. "Do you have any other plans after school?"

Sure, rub it in. I shift my backpack from one shoulder to the other, hesitating. There's a *reason* I don't involve myself in extracurricular activities. "Um..."

"Don't pressure her." Mara gives his arm a shove and then turns to me. "It's okay, London. You can say no. But if you change your mind just swing by the drama room, yeah?"

"Sure," I say, but the three of them are already walking off, leaving me standing in the nearly empty hall with a Hello Kitty pen and no idea of what just happened.

It isn't that they aren't good people. Mara's a sweetheart. Wade is quiet, but he's known for being Mister Nice Guy. Trevor can be a little forward but he's goofy and Mara obviously likes him. It isn't that I don't love drama, because I do. I put serious thought into joining freshman year but I couldn't bring myself to do it. Too much had changed and my heart wasn't dedicated to being *me* in a school that wanted everyone to fall in line and be the same. High school is nothing like junior high. Junior high involved me being bold and bright and outgoing. Here at Maple Burrow, it's all about blending in and keeping my head down.

Still...I won't say the offer isn't tempting.

Jasmine isn't outside when I reach the parking lot. No surprise there. There's a text waiting for me on my cell: *Catching a ride to Dad's. See you at home.*

My nose crinkles. I toss the phone to the passenger's seat and buckle in. I love my little sister but it doesn't mean I have to like her a lot of the time. Or her stupid-ass decisions. Like who she hangs out with, or how much time she spends with Dad. Whatever. We've had that argument until we were both blue in the face and I'm not up for it again. It's Friday, the weather is rainy and perfect.

And tomorrow, I get to attend my first pride event.

2

I've skipped four other pride celebrations near my city in the last two years. Over the summer there was a parade downtown; I drove there, parked, and never got out of the car. I kept thinking, *What if someone from school sees me and then everyone knows?* It's still a legitimate fear but I've pressed it to the far recesses of my brain in an effort not to dwell on it. Dwelling never got anyone anywhere except in a shrink's office.

Besides, I'm a senior in high school. Only a few months left of keeping a low profile before I can graduate and get the hell out of here...right? You can sure bet I'll be going to a college that couldn't care less how I dress, the color of my hair, or whether I'm interested in boys, girls, or anything in between.

I've still taken precautions by sporting a pair of sunglasses and a cap over my messy hair. I've worn the plainest getup I could manage with my otherwise colorful closet that didn't involve wearing my school uniform, borrowed a pair of sneakers from Mom, and here I am. Ready to mingle. Ready to *blend.*

This is a fundraising pride thing-a-ma-bob, a fall celebratory event. Some carnival games, vendors, food, a pumpkin patch, all to raise money for the city's LGBT group which really consists of maybe six individuals who are bound and determined to stay afloat despite the lack of support from our primarily conservative community.

There is no real point in me being here. I'm not trying to meet people or pick someone up. But meandering through the stalls and stopping to collect a pamphlet here and there, I can't help but think this is the first time in my life I've been able to relax around others who are like me. No, it's not even that. *Like me?* It's not that at all. I see some guys and girls walking hand-in-hand or parents here and there, supporting their kids. What I wanted wasn't a group of people *like* me, but a group of people who *accept* me. A place where I don't have to avert my eyes and keep my head down so I don't get noticed.

A girl at one of the vendor booths hands me a business card for the only gay bar downtown. I give her a cheeky grin and offer it back. "I've got a few years before they'll let me in."

"They do have an under twenty-one night," she says. "What's your name?"

Before getting here, I had planned on using an alias if anyone asked. The idea completely slips my mind now. "London." I offer my hand which she grips and gives a shake. She introduces herself and tells me to stop by the bar to say hi sometime. Could be she's interested. Could be she's just doing her job as an employee and trying to lure in customers. Either way, I walk away feeling pleased with myself for interacting.

I never had a problem talking to people growing up. Then I hit high school and suddenly keeping quiet became a means of survival. I had been in the process of grieving being separated from my two best friends from middle school and making new friends wasn’t something that came easy anymore. Not in a small, stifled place like Maple Burrow.

After meeting the bar employee, opening up becomes easier. I chat with two guys who were childhood best friends that hooked up their junior year. I meet people who've been out for years and others who, like me, haven't told a soul. People are welcoming. People are warm. People are nonjudgmental.

My nerves were running amuck this morning and made me skip breakfast, so I stop at a cart near the parking lot to grab a sandwich and something hot to drink. I take a seat at a vacant picnic table outside of the hustle and bustle to enjoy my food; I have this thing against eating in my car. Crumbs and all that. Besides, I want to enjoy the atmosphere for awhile longer before going home.

From here I can see couples of all sorts coming and going, and I think...this is cool. This is good. I wish school could be like this. Hell, I wish the whole world could be like this. 'The Gay' is not infectious, the world is not coming to an end, and people are happy. Gosh, how about that. Look at that guy, there. On his own just like me. Even he looks content as he's headed for the parking lot. Funny, he looks a lot like Wade from school. I squint, lifting my sunglasses.

Holy crap. That doesn't just look like Wade, it *is* Wade.

First thought: sheer panic. What if he sees me?

Second thought: *wait..* If Wade is here, if Wade was wandering around, then it means one of two things; either he's gay, or he's fine with people who are.

A surge of bravery (idiocy?) drives me out of my seat to go after him, discarding the remains of my lunch in the trash and hoisting my purse over my shoulder. Wade is moving at a brisk pace but I manage to catch up to him in the parking lot. I even recognize his green pickup parked a few spots down from my ancient Dodge Raider.

"Wade!"

There's a hitch in his steps, a stiffening of his shoulders. He stops just shy of the driver's side door, head turning. His expression falls to the asphalt when he sees me.

"Hey." I halt a few feet away. "How's it going? Were you here for the carnival?"

"Just passing through," Wade says tightly, jamming the key into the door and making every effort to avoid eye-contact.

It takes everything I have to keep my smile in place. Is he lying? I can think of twenty different reasons why he would. Then again, he could be telling the truth and I've just shot myself in the foot approaching him with such a question. Too late to back down now.

"It was fun," I offer. "Good food, too. I've never been to this sort of thing before, but—"

"*London.*" The sharpness of his tone startles me to silence. Wade braces his hands against his open truck door and the roof, dragging in a deep breath. "I was only passing through. That's all." He looks at me finally, catching my gaze and holding it. "Got it?"

That phrase in of itself should sound intimidating. Instead all I see is the panic in Wade's eyes and hear the desperation in his tone. I realize that Wade is me a few years back, where even the mere idea that I was different made me feel wrong. Placed alongside the fact that Wade is well-liked, popular, and has a slew of girls at school who would line up to jump his bones, I can't say I blame him for freaking out a little.

Still, any words I think to say have caught in my throat. All I can do is offer him a mute nod and a forced smile. Of course I won't tell. I'm not that kind of person, and Wade has never been unkind to me to warrant me spilling his secret.

Wade nods once. He gets into his car and takes off out of the parking lot. I don't know what to feel. Saddened because of that look in his eyes, or relieved because I'm not as alone as I thought I was.

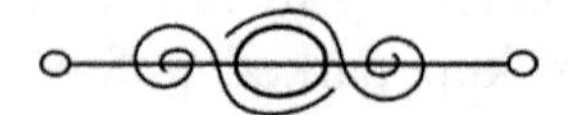

Mom is finishing up dinner in her work clothes when I get home. I don't have the heart to tell her I've already eaten so I take a seat at the table and watch her flit about the kitchen from stove to cupboards to fridge and back again.

She asks, "Did you have fun today?"

"Yeah, sure." I prop my chin in my hands. "Aside from the weekend crowds." At the movies. Because that's totally where I was.

I hate lying to Mom, but I'll admit I have a knack for it. Jasmine is the horrible liar.

Speak of the devil... Jazz whisks into the room, applying lipstick as she goes. That's my sister, the multi-tasker.

"I don't get you," she says, plunking her purse onto the table. "Going to the movies by yourself? That's kind of sad."

There is no serious malice in her tone but it doesn't keep me from retorting, "Not as sad as painting yourself up like a hooker for a bunch of girls who only like you because you pretend to be a rich snob."

"Girls," Mom warns. Jazz shoots me a murderous look, dropping the lipstick into her purse.

I don't stop. "Really, though. Do they hiss and make the sign of the cross when they come to pick you up and see the apartment?"

"I'm meeting them there." She turns away, apparently done with trying to converse with me, and lets Mom give her a kiss on the cheek.

"Keep your phone on. Home by eleven."

Jazz waves dismissively as she ducks out the door. Is she taking a bus to a friend's house so she doesn't let anyone see her home? Nice. Real nice. Her friends know she doesn't live in some big condo or townhouse. But as far as I'm aware, she's never brought any of them over. It's like this thing they just don't talk about. I guess we're an embarrassment.

"You really don't need to be so hard on her," Mom tsks. I push my chair back and stand to get out plates and glasses. "She's a freshman. She's getting to explore this whole social scene for the first time."

"It's a stupid scene," I mutter, setting our places at the table. "Pretending to be something you're not just to fit in."

"Sort of like pretending to be something you're not so you *don't* fit in." Mom turns off the burners and swivels to face me, one eyebrow cocked.

Heat rushes to my face. "What's that supposed to mean?"

"You used to have friends, London. Jasmine says you don't talk to anyone at school. You won't join any of the clubs or extracurricular activities to meet people." A small crease forms between her brows. "You've spent the last three years telling me everything was full and had no room for you, but Jazz says—"

"Jazz says a lot of things and should mind her own business." I plop back into my chair. "I'm not interested, Mom. I don't feel like dealing with it. You see Jazz. Every other day so-and-so and what's-her-name are fighting or getting together or breaking up. It's stupid." That isn't a total lie. I *do* hate the rumors and the gossip, but what Mom said rings true. I'm as much of a fake as Jasmine is. Our goals are just different. She wants to be accepted and loved. I want to be invisible so I can survive with my heart and confidence still intact.

Mom heaves a sigh that signals the end of the conversation. She worries. I know she does. She's making up for the fact that Dad is hardly in our lives (well, not in my life, anyway) and that she has to be a mom *and* a dad. I wish I knew how to tell her that having just a mom is totally fine with me because Dad can go play in traffic for all I care.

Instead, I eat dinner with her in silence. When she leaves for work, she gives me a tight hug and murmurs, "I worry about you, sweetheart, but you know I love you just how you are."

In that moment, I think I could tell her about so many things. Like how lonely I get and how much I want to fit in but that I'm scared and I hate my school. Maybe about how I miss her ever since Dad left, because she's been working so much and I'm always home alone. Like how Jasmine has become a stranger to me in recent months, or...

Mom pauses, tilts her head. "You all right?"

Nothing I'm feeling could possibly overcome the guilt I would feel at dumping my problems on Mom. So I swallow it all down and force my mouth into something that wants to be a smile when it grows up. "Yeah, of course. I'm fine."

3

Diary of a Noble

What would society at large think if there was a "heterosexual pride event"? If a gaggle of straight people gathered to celebrate their straightness, or to show support for heterosexuality?

People would probably think they were homophobic. It's sort of like the whole Black History Month, and how if there were a White History Month people would scream racism.

I'm not sure how to word why it's different, but maybe it is. Maybe because every other day of the year seems like a heterosexual pride event? Straight people and their ability to hold hands in public without being side-eyed. Their ability to get married in every state, to file taxes together, to receive health benefits without question...

So maybe it's fair, then, that we get little moments to shine all on our own. It was pretty awesome getting to be a part of the celebration this time around. For the very first time, I was able to walk through a crowd and have them know my secret without being afraid of the consequences.

And to see *W* there? I'm not sure what to make of that. I had hoped...

Oh, geez. I don't know what I hoped.

I desperately want to believe I am not alone.

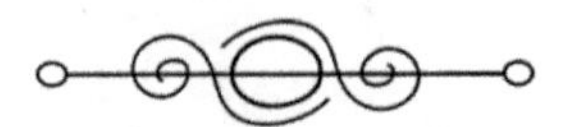

Jasmine is never at her best on Monday mornings; most people aren't. But this Monday she's in an especially pissy mood, glaring at her Fruit Loops like they've caused her some grave offense. When we get into the car to leave for school, she slams the door with more force than is necessary. Given her fluctuating moods and how easy it is to send her spiraling into a meltdown, it might be nicer for me to keep my mouth shut and leave her alone.

Or not. "Someone forget their happy pills this morning?" When you live with a person for fifteen years, you get over the urge to always be nice.

Jazz casts me a scathing look, folding her arms and hunching down in her seat like she's worried someone driving by will see her. "Shut up."

"Seriously. What's your deal? You've been a bitch all weekend."

"You're a bitch. It's really none of your business."

"Nice comeback," I say dryly. I try to think back to when I was her age. Can't say that I was ever such a jerk—especially to my sister.

I miss those days. I miss middle school. I miss Delaine and Lisa, because they were my whole world back then and I don't exist to them anymore. Jazz and I got along. Of course, Dad was also around so we were a complete family. We were whole.

A thought dawns on me as I pull into the school parking lot. "Is it Dad?"

Jazz's reaction is subtle. A tilt of her shoulder. A casual flick of her hand to tuck her blonde hair behind an ear. Overly casual, in fact. "Oh, you care about Dad now?"

"Nope. I was asking if he did or said something that upset you." I take my time picking a spot, hoping to keep her confined to the car a few minutes longer. "You went over there the other day."

"Really none of your business. If you want to know what's going on with Dad, maybe you should pick up the phone and call him." With the car still rolling at a pleasant two miles an hour, Jasmine throws open the door. She stumbles getting out as I slam on the brakes, and then stalks off, forgetting her purse. Which means she's going to be in an even worse mood come this afternoon because she won't degrade herself enough to seek me out for the car keys during school hours.

I watch her go. Things between us used to be pretty good. So what happened? At what precise moment did we become such different people with different wants? When was the first time she shot me down when I invited her to hang out with her big sister?

No idea. I feel guilty for that because I know it has to be partly my fault. And I can't in good conscience leave her purse behind. Not without rifling through it to see if her meds are still in there. If she isn't carting them around in her backpack, she's going to need them whether she wants to see me or not.

I find the anxiety meds. Or rather, I find the bottle. Frowning, I pull it out and peer inside. Empty. Just last week I took her to fill the prescription with a thirty day supply and the date on the bottle matches up. Bizarre. Maybe she put them in a baggy in her backpack or something. Still, I bring her purse with me.

I don't have a chance to see her until lunch. Approaching her while she's eating in one of the courtyards with her friends might be what she deserves for going off on me, and I put serious consideration into it, but ultimately...I find myself at her locker, trying to remember her combination. It's only one number off from mine. As I'm fussing with it, a locker a few spots down slams shut and makes me jump.

"That's not your locker," Wade says.

I twist around to peer at him. "Oh. Uh. No, it belongs to Jasmine. My sister."

Wade gives me an appraising look, lifting an eyebrow. No wonder Jazz came home her very first day of high school with a dreamy sigh and a comment about how handsome he was. He's got one of those faces that gets cuter the longer you look at him. "I didn't know she was your sister."

I give him a rakish grin then duck my head to continue messing with the lock. "That doesn't surprise me."

"Oh." Silence. He scratches the back of his head. "What are you doing with your sister's locker, exactly?"

"She forgot her purse," I explain. "God forbid I try to give it to her where people will see us within ten feet of each other."

"She's in my art class right after lunch. I could give it to her?"

That gives me pause. I tilt my head, gaze sliding to the left. Jazz will be pissed I gave her purse to Wade of all people, but I'm not really at the point of caring right now.

"You know, that'd be great." I let her lock thunk against the door and offer the purse to Wade with a smile. "You're super. Thanks."

Then I turn to leave and Wade stops me by saying, "I'm sorry, by the way."

I slowly twirl on my heel. "Hm?"

"I'm sorry," he repeats, looking awkward and adorable with his backpack hanging from one hand and Jasmine's baby blue purse from the other. "About the other day. I shouldn't have snapped at you like that."

I'm inclined to agree. "No, you shouldn't have. But whatever." Shrug. "Don't go thinking I'm going to run my mouth to anyone. I doubt they'd believe me, anyway."

"I'm not worried." He frowns. A couple of girls pass by, they side-eye us with furrowed brows as they marvel at a Nobody talking with Wade Jones. He doesn't help matters by flicking his gaze to them and promptly moving in closer. To avoid being overheard, no doubt, but from an outsider's perspective it has to look suspect.

"Look...I don't want you getting the wrong idea, is all. I'm not—and I've never—"

I hold up my hands to cut him off. "Whatever you want to keep secret is your deal, all right? I'm not here to tell you off because of your preferences of...whatever."

"I'm not gay," he says urgently.

I level a stare at him. "Never said you were."

He takes a deep breath. In, out again. "Are you?"

"Not really any of your business."

"Then you're hiding just as much as I am."

I hike my backpack further up my aching shoulder and finally take a step back, putting some distance between us. It isn't the same at all. If someone were to ask me flat-out, I don't think I could deny it. I'm simply not offering the information, right? The one time I did, I regretted it. But I know Wade is scared and I can't honestly blame him. "Like I said, Wade. I'm not saying a word if you're not. But if you ever want to talk about it, I'll catch you around."

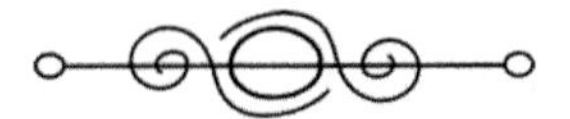

Jasmine flings herself into the car at the end of the day with the fury of a hurricane. I hadn't expected she'd be catching a ride home with me since she so rarely does anymore. The less time she spends at home, the happier she is. She throws her backpack into the back seat and hunkers down. "I can't believe you."

She has her purse in her hands. That makes me smile. I start up the car and head out of the parking lot through bumper-to-bumper traffic. "What did I do?"

"You gave my purse to *Wade*, of all people? What were you thinking?"

"I was thinking you needed your medicine," I drawl. Jazz fidgets. I'm tempted to ask where all her pills went, but think better of it. "What's the big deal? You always wanted a reason to talk to him. I gave you one."

"Yeah, and now all my friends in art know you're my sister," she says. "Wade announced—rather loudly—that he got the purse from you."

My grip tightens on the wheel. "They had to have known that I'm your sister." I always knew Jazz didn't talk much about her home life and that she refuses to be seen with me. But has she really, seriously, *never* told them who I was? Or even that she had a sibling? We look related. Not to mention, hello? Same last name?

Jazz studies me, tight-lipped, arms crossed, then whips her head away to stare out the frosty window. "Only, like, two of them knew. And now that everyone else has been told, good luck blending in because they're going to start noticing you. Congratulations."

"Oh *shut up*, Jazz. Don't act like you pretended to be an only child because you were doing me a favor when you were just protecting your own precious reputation. Maybe you wouldn't freak out so much about what other people think if you were taking your medication like you're supposed to."

"Stop the car."

"I mean, seriously? We *just* filled that prescription. What are you doing? Tossing it down the drain? Mom's not made of money."

"Stop. The. Car."

"And I'm the one driving you to all your appointments. If you're not even going to bother, then—"

"STOP THE CAR!"

I wrench the wheel to one side, bringing us half an inch from the curb at an odd angle. Maybe I shouldn't let her out; maybe I should tell her I'm sorry and to stop being overdramatic because it's cold and wet outside. She throws open the door and gets out, slams it, and starts off down the street. I shouldn't let her.

No. You know what? Fuck her. My feelings are hurt. I always accommodate her wishes to not be seen with me. I never approach her at school, I never try to talk to her friends or make myself known. I am the sister that does not exist.

I watch her huffing down the road, arms still folded and curls bouncing. The colors of her clothes blur together, blue to pink to the blonde of her hair. How ridiculous am I, sitting here crying over something so stupid? Am I really that embarrassing of a sister to have? Why? Just because I'm not popular?

I wipe harshly at my eyes. By the time I'm driving again I don't see Jasmine anywhere, which means she either hitched a ride with someone passing by, got on a bus, or went to a friend's. Either way, I'm not going to worry myself over it. I head straight home. If Jazz doesn't want me as a sister, why should I bother acting like one?

4

Mom isn't home. No surprise there. The empty apartment is torture, its silence all-encompassing and way too depressing for my liking. I keep waiting to hear the front door open, signaling Jazz's undoubtedly displeasured entrance, but...nothing.

In the silence I drag my laptop to the living room, finish up some homework I didn't get to during classes, browse around online, and reply to a few messages and emails. It isn't entirely true that I don't have friends, it just so happens most of my friends live far away. Southern California, Chicago, the UK, Australia. We don't usually talk about anything of substance, but we are all brought together by our love for movies and TV shows, books, celebrities, and fictional characters. Escapism. Not totally healthy, but it beats the alternative. We are those joined by social awkwardness and either a lack of interest in 'real-life' friends, or the inability to make them. I guess I fall somewhere in between.

By eight, it's dark outside and most of my East coast friends have gone to bed. The weight of my loneliness has become exhausting. I think about what Wade said earlier, how I'm hiding as much as he is, and I wonder if he's right. I mean, I am hiding from everyone else, but not from myself, so isn't that different? Isn't accepting myself all I have to do? Or is hiding from the world—even my own family—not being true to myself because I don't have the faith even my mother and sister will accept me? My best friends turned their backs on me. That was bad enough. Jasmine is already embarrassed of me; I can imagine her face if I tried to tell her I'm a lesbian and I've spent the last year and a half crushing on Mara Nitesh. Yeah. Sure. That'd go over great.

The longer I sit here the more I'm going to dwell on all this crap, and dwelling isn't something I care to do. It's eight o'clock, Mom is gone for the night, who knows if Jasmine is coming back anytime soon, I'm starving and not about to go through the effort of cooking dinner for just me again. Nevermind that going out to get food will take about the same amount of time and effort, but whatever. I scribble a note for Jazz because I don't feel like texting, grab my coat and wallet, and hop into the car. I have ten bucks in my pocket. Mom is working at the diner, so why not drop by?

It's a bit of a drive to Bruno's Diner but the soft pitter-patter of rain against the windshield in the dark is soothing. By the time I arrive, I'm thinking a little clearer and my emotions aren't threatening to make my brain explode.

The other employees know me by now. It's typical for only two waitresses to be here during weeknights. Wanda spots me and we exchange waves as I take a booth closest to the kitchen. While I'm waiting, I check my cell to find a text from Jasmine: *Staying at Dad's.* Well, super-duper for her. I absolutely hate staying home alone all night and she knows it, but whatever.

Mom is across the diner, taking orders from a couple at the counter. She disappears in back to put in their ticket and reappears a moment later, wiping her hands on her apron as she wanders over. "Hey, sweetheart. I didn't know you were stopping by."

I shrug. "Surprise?"

She tips her head and sooths her palm over my hair. She smells like yummy, greasy french fries. "Definitely. What can I get for you?"

"Surprise me." I grin a little. Once upon a time Dad, Jasmine, and I would come here to visit Mom a few times a week. She could get us a discount on food. At the time it was the coolest thing ever. Looking back, I wonder if it was laziness on Dad's part, an inability to be an adult and prepare meals for us seeing as he wasn't doing anything else useful.

Mom says, "You got it," and vanishes again. I don't see her until she returns with a basket of chicken strips and fries and a healthy helping of barbeque sauce. And, oh, hallelujah—she brings me a chocolate shake to top it all off.

"You're awesome."

"I know." Mom kisses the top of my head. "Are you sure there's nothing wrong? You don't usually come here anymore."

One of the fries finds its new home in my mouth. Chewing and swallowing gives me a few extra seconds to formulate a convincing response. "Jazz went to Dad's." Ooh, I'm a tattle-tale. The brief flicker of pain across Mom's face makes me regret it, too.

"Well...she does that sometimes. No surprise."

"It's stupid." I scoop sauce onto another fry, watching it drip off the end. "She's stupid."

"She's your sister. Don't say things like that."

"I can say she's stupid *because* she's my sister. I don't understand the point of hanging around someone who has hurt you and your family as much as Dad has."

Mom heaves a world-weary sigh and slides into the booth across from me. "London... The age difference may not seem like much, but Jasmine wasn't as old as you when all of that happened. She's held on to the happier memories. It doesn't help that you've always been an obnoxiously perceptive child; you caught onto the problems more than she did."

I frown into my food. That statement doesn't seem even remotely true. At least, I don't feel like I knew anything. If I had, couldn't I have done something to stop it?

"My point being," Mom continues, resting her hand on my arm, "is that you and Jasmine deal with things very differently. I try to respect both of your decisions in having a relationship with your father—or not, in your case—and I wish the two of you would do the same for each other."

She gets nothing but a grunt out of me in response so she sighs, pats my arm, and gets back to work.

I take my time eating, but there is only so long I can drag it out without looking ridiculous. Mom doesn't bring me a ticket so I suspect she got the meal on the house, meaning I get to pocket my ten bucks. Even with a full stomach, I don't want to go home to an empty apartment. For the next hour I walk around downtown in the dark. Since I don't have anyone to talk to, I try to talk things through with myself instead.

I don't enjoy being this way, so completely alone when I really want to be around someone. Gone are the days of middle school when I had people to call any hour of the day or night if I wanted, and my phone was always ringing. Maybe I didn't have a ton of friends, but I had great ones. Sometimes I'm envious of Jasmine. Sometimes I wish I had what it took to be someone outgoing and charismatic so others would gravitate toward me like Mara.

It's October. Nine months lay between me and graduation, and although my grades have been stellar and I won't have too many difficulties being accepted into a college, I still feel like...what have I *really* accomplished in high school? No friends. No extracurricular activities. No school dances. Nothing worth telling my kids about someday. And I have no one to blame but myself. I've distanced myself, I've laid low and kept my eyes on the ground.

Nine months. Is there enough time to change that? I mean, a baby can be grown in nine months. Why can't I grow, too?

By the time I reach the car again and drive home, it's later than I meant for it to be. Mom won't be back until the early hours of morning and Jazz is still gone. At this exact moment, though? I don't care. I fire off a text to Mom to say goodnight and thanks for dinner. She won't be able to text back until her lunch break, so I won't wait up. Home is empty and eerie, but that's okay. I'm going to work myself out of this depression. I'm going to write.

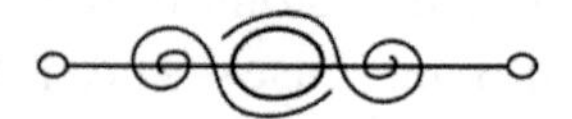

Diary of a Noble

There is something to be said for last-minute decisions. Deciding to attend a party twenty minutes before it starts and then meeting your new best friend when you arrive. Deciding to grab that lottery ticket because what the hell, why not? Then hearing your winning numbers called.

Deciding that even though you've tried so hard to get through high school unnoticed, maybe it wasn't the best decision and this is not how you want to be remembered. I don't want to look back and think these years were completely wasted because I was afraid.

I don’t want to be my sister, being someone else just so people know my name. No, I simply want to be me. I want friends who will know my favorite color, the bands I like, my preference of the Tenth Doctor over the Eleventh, how Sunday nights are reserved for all my favorite TV shows, and how I have no problem waiting in line for the midnight release of a video game I've had on pre-order for months. I want people to know these things about me, and to love me regardless.

I think I just described my mom. Sigh.

My point being, I still have this year to change things. It's only October. I've been thinking all night how I will go about this and I have made a decision. I will go back to my roots. I will find something that once made me happy and see if it still has the same effect.

I am going to join drama.

My choice to pick up an after-school activity isn't as spur-of-the-moment as it sounds. I was in theater in middle school and loved it. My teacher said I had the perfect personality for it: a strong projecting voice, and a knack for memorizing lines and making them my own. Granted that was years ago, but here's hoping I'm not too rusty.

Who is in the drama club? Mara.

And her boyfriend. And Wade.

But still—Mara.

I'm not holding my breath for something magical to happen. I've simply decided if I'm going through this not-blending thing, I want to get to know her as a friend. A person is still fascinating whether you're with them romantically or not and I don't want to look back ten years from now and wonder why I never even had the nerve to strike up a conversation with her.

Doesn't make it any easier when I walk into the theater room after school and all eyes turn to me. I know some of these people from classes. Others from passing in the halls. I know a few names, but not all. I pay attention to those around me but I'm getting enough blank expressions that it's safe to say most of these people have never even glanced my way. Mr. Cobb, the drama teacher, isn't here yet.

I stand in the doorway with an awkward smile on my face. "Hello drama club."

Wade, bless him, gets up from where he was seated on the edge of the stage to rescue me. "London? What're you doing here?"

Several pairs of eyes are suddenly regarding me with a lot more interest. Gasp! *Wade knows me.* I'm a nobody who is speaking to Wade. This is way more attention than I'm comfortable with, but I'm going to have to get used to it if I want to go through with this whole thing.

"I was hoping to talk to Mr. Cobb about joining." I step into the room like I'm entering a minefield. "If it's not too late in the year, I mean. You guys mentioned needing more people."

Wade stops a few feet from me, hands in his pockets. He throws a glance back in the direction of his friends and shrugs. "Uh, I don't think it's too late."

"We always have room for more," Mara offers, sliding from Trevor's side to approach. "We usually have to double-up on parts and come in on weekends to get sets done."

Trevor laughs. "Don't chase her off." He gives me a wave.

You'd think I'd be insanely jealous of this guy, but he seems nice enough so I just smile and wiggle my fingers.

From behind me, Mr. Cobb steps through the door. I inch to the side to make room for him. "Afternoon! Running a bit behind today, sorry. Everyone, let's get into your groups and talk to your writers about their scripts." His gaze sweeps over the room and settles on me. "Can I help you?"

I open my mouth, but Mara cuts me off. "This is London and she wants to join the club. Can she?"

Mr. Cobb purses his lips, looking around again. Everyone is assembling into groups of five or six, four groups total aside from Trevor, Wade, Mara, and a girl I recognize from the last few years who was sitting with them. "Well..."

Mara says, "She can be in our group. We only have four."

"Yes, that's fine. London, is it?" He pats me on the back. "Make sure you fill out a form at the office and have your parents sign it."

I don't explain to him that I'm eighteen and already filled out my own permission form. Mr. Cobb is moving away to start talking to each of the groups. Mara beams and latches her arms around one of mine, tugging me toward where they were previously huddled on the stage. "You don't mind being in our group, do you, London?"

I look down at our arms, sinking to the stage with her. "Uh, what? No. What are we doing?"

The other girl in the group—Amber, I remember her name is—has glasses and her light brown hair pulled into a messy ponytail. She's reading over papers that look a lot like a script. "Mr. Cobb has each group organizing their own production. Scripts, sets, acting, the whole nine yards." Amber nods at Wade. "He's our script writer. I'm in charge of sets and costumes."

"Not that she knows a thing about making costumes," Trevor says. Amber gives him a sour look.

Mara is still holding onto my arm but I manage to focus enough to reply, "I can help with costumes. I have a sewing machine."

"There you go, Amber." Wade has settled on the other side of me, legs crossed, elbows on his knees. "We're pretty new into the whole process. The script isn't even finished. I'll get you a copy of what I have and we'll figure out a role for you to play...assuming you want a role."

That seems like a silly thing to say. I give him a lopsided grin. "I'm here, aren't I?

6

Mara brings a copy of the incomplete script to my locker the next morning. I manage to get away with walking her all the way to her first period class because she's chatting about costume ideas. Wade's script is a dark comedy set in the 1800's about a wife finding out her husband is cheating on her with a prostitute. Even skimming through the first few pages, I can see that Wade has some natural talent as a writer. Not something you'd know by looking at him.

Trevor has the role of the husband. Mara, the wife. Which makes me raise an eyebrow because—"So I'm supposed to be the hooker?"

Mara laughs and playfully hits my arm. "It's a really great part, though. She has the best lines. Give it a read and let us know what you think this afternoon?"

My first role. The first time anyone in school will take note of me, and it'll be playing a whore. All righty. I said I was going to do this and I'm not going to back down now.

I spend my lunch reading through the script. It really is good, and Mara was right. Mable—the prostitute—has some of the best lines in the play. It's funny, if you've got a morbid sense of humor. I can already imagine costumes in my head. I'll need references for the time period, but that's not a problem.

As I'm reading a shadow falls across the page, blocking my light. I squint. I know that silhouette.

"Hi, sister," I say.

"What are you doing?" It's not a *what are you doing right this minute* so much as a *what the hell do you think you're doing in a general sense of the word.*

I lean back, folding my hands together. "Reading. What are you doing?"

"I meant about drama," Jasmine says. "You were never interested in it before. Now you're being all buddy-buddy with Wade?"

"Wow. It's really not like that. And what are you talking about? I've always loved drama."

Jazz studies me through slit eyes, hands on her narrow hips. I'm honestly surprised she's not throwing more of a fit. I'll take mild annoyance over unbridled fury any day. "You haven't done anything the last four years at this school. What made you change your mind?"

My shoulders lift and fall in a shrug. "I had a long talk with a friend." Myself, but that counts.

"You don't have any friends."

Ow. Okay, I'll let that slide. "I came to the conclusion that I need to do less blending and spend this year doing something memorable."

Jazz is silent a moment before sinking onto the bench beside me. "I've never really gotten that."

"Hm?"

"You. Blending, or whatever you call it."

"You do the same thing. You go out of your way to be noticed. I go out of my way not to be. We're both just pretending to be something we're not. I've decided that isn't what I want to do anymore."

She has no response for that. She swings her legs idly and studies her hands in her lap, and that she's still here reminds me that she *never* approaches me at school—even out here, in this quad where no one will see us—unless she really wants something. Here I thought we were bonding. Sigh.

"What do you want?"

"Can you take me to the pharmacy after school?" she mutters.

Of course. "They're not going to fill your prescription again when you just got it filled."

"I already talked to my doctor and told him I lost them. It's been filled."

"But you didn't lose them." I give up on the idea I'll be getting any more reading done. The script is tucked carefully back into its folder and then my backpack. "So where did they go?"

"Please, London, can you just...not ask questions?" Jasmine sighs. "I pinky swear I'm not taking them like candy. I'm not Dad."

Jazz is a shitty liar so I know she's telling the truth. Maybe she really did lose them. Maybe she spilled them. All I know is she needs my help, and just this once, I guess I can accommodate her to calm the waters between us.

I pat her leg and stand. "I have drama club. If you want to wait around, I'll take you after."

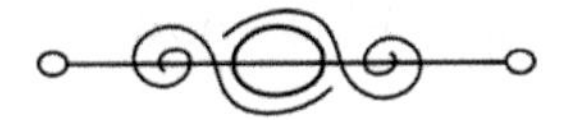

Mara is waiting for me when I get to the theater after school. She hops to her feet, startling a sleepy-looking Trevor beside her, all smiles. "London!" She waves at me like I'm not ten feet away and can't see her just fine. "Have you thought about it?"

I take a seat between her and Amber. "Thought about...?"

"The role! Will you do it?"

"Oh." I unzip my backpack to take out my copy of the incomplete script. "Yeah. I mean, I figured it was a given." Meaning I didn't think I really had a choice. I came here to get involved. To act. Not to sit around on my ass.

Mara smacks Wade lightly on the knee. "There you go! We have our Mable."

Wade casts me a sidelong look that I can't decipher. Something between *I think you're fucking nuts* and *I hope you know what you're doing.* I hope I do, too. That expression of his makes me doubt my ability to do this at all. I haven't acted since a condensed version of Romeo and Juliet in the eighth grade. Not exactly a huge credit on my record.

"I'll get the script finished up this weekend," Wade says.

Mara rubs her hands against her jeans. "Great! Then why don't Trevor, Amber, and I work more on the sets and you two can talk about costumes?"

Seems like an innocent enough suggestion. Except then Mara winks at me. She *winks*. Like being left alone with Wade is this huge favor she's doing because...why? What? How? I'm clearly missing something here but I'm not in the position to ask, *Hey, what was that? Got something in your eye?*

Besides, she and Amber are already relocating to the far back of the stage where other groups are busy at work on cardboard cutouts and painting scenery. Amber throws a glance over her shoulder and cocks an eyebrow. Another look I don't begin to understand.

Wade ducks his head, fishing a few printed images from his drama folder. I lean over slowly. "Does Mara think I have a thing for you?"

He doesn't look up. "Who knows? She likes trying to play match-maker with me."

"Maybe because you haven't had a girlfriend all year."

"Since freshman year, thank you very much."

"Oh, because that's less suspicious."

"I don't honestly care at this point, London." Wade slides the pictures to me. "I only have a few months. I don't have time for a relationship. College apps and school keep me busy."

I hmm, flipping through the pages of men and women in their pretty attire, setting aside a few I can use as reference for making our own. Mostly, though, mulling over what Wade just said; it's as close to a confession as I'm likely to get from him. "Mmhm. This one here—not going to work at all. Doesn't fit the time period. And this one's a bit too complicated."

Wade is listening, but his eyes are all squinched up like he's trying to figure me out. "Why do you do that?"

My eyebrows lift. "Do what?"

"Change the subject."

"I thought you didn't want to talk about it? You bit my head off the last two times I tried."

Wade falls silent and I think I get it. He *does* want to talk, but he's gotten so used to keeping his mouth shut and minding what he says around everyone all the time that he doesn't know how without someone prying it out of him. I know this, because

I'm the exact same way. Hell, maybe I'm not pushing him because I'm not sure how to talk about it myself.

Which is precisely why I drop the subject again. No comments. No pushing. Wade doesn't try to ask about it but I find myself being more aware of him. Of his movements, his expressions. His shoulders are always squared and a little tense, his mouth downturned. Even when he smiles, his brows are still twitched together in a faint frown, like he's smiling because he knows it's the social norm and not because he feels it. His eyes are...sad? I don't know. I'm far from the first person who should be making assumptions on a person and their personal life, but...

I do wonder what Wade's family is like and what they would say if they found out he's gay. What would change for him if his secret got out? For that matter, when did he realize he liked guys? Was it a gradual realization? Was it recent? Was he young? All these things cross my mind over the next hour until it's time to pack up and go home. I've come to the conclusion if either of us wants to talk, maybe some of those questions are the way to start off. Maybe I'll have to talk first. I can do that. I think. Can't I?

Before leaving, I write down my cell number on one of the rejected costume references, fold it up, and slip it into his hand. "In case you want to talk," I say. "About the costumes or...you know. Whatever." Him. Me. Us. The world.

I can feel Wade's eyes on my back the entire time I'm calling goodbye to the others and heading out the door. I don't know if that's a good thing or not, or if he'll call or casually lose my number in the first trash can. An effort was made and I put myself out there a bit.

Jasmine is waiting by the car because God forbid she be near the theater where someone might see us together. She's texting someone on her cell, but pockets it when she spots me. She frowns. "What're you smiling for?"

"Am I?" I hadn't realized I was. "Oh, I don't know. Something Wade said." The look on her face is payback for treating me like a social pariah at school. She desperately wants to ask about Wade, maybe ask if we talk about her or if I *like* him but even if she does, I'm not going to say a word. She can squirm for awhile.

We stop by the pharmacy and I stay parked while Jazz runs inside to get her medication. I make her take one right there in the car even though it means her swallowing it dry, and by the time we're nearing home she's mellowed out some. She's a little more like the Jazz I remember. Less like a wound-up clock ready to bust its gears.

In fact, she's calmed down enough that we actually stop for fast food to have dinner together. Greasy cheeseburgers and fries and a huge milkshake to share that will fill my poor stomach with regret later, but tastes delicious now. I ask where she got the money for this and she says Dad gave her twenty bucks last time she saw him. I hmm at that, but don't question it.

Last I heard Dad wasn't exactly doing so hot in terms of finances. It was part of what ruined things between him and Mom. All the money from his job as a legal secretary went to drugs. Weed, crack, pills, whatever he could get. Then he got found out, was fired not just because he was taking the drugs but because he was buying and selling them to and from clients. He's a lucky fuck that he was never arrested for it. After that, he took to working whatever office jobs he could get but they weren't lasting long. Either he'd fail the drug tests, they'd catch him coming to work completely off his rocker, or he'd vanish for days on end and not show up at all.

I don't know what he's doing now. I don't know if rehab worked like Jazz said it did, if he's really cleaned up enough to hold a job that enables him to drop twenty bucks into his daughter's hand when she asks for it. Not my business. I've detached myself from him, and that includes whatever happens between him and Jazz. That was the promise I made to myself for her sake as well as my own.

I'm not about to let it ruin our evening together. This is the first nice time we've had since she started high school.

We stay up until Mom comes home close to midnight. Although she gives us the most exasperated look that we aren't in bed, she's fighting back a smile that must be because we're hanging out together. She changes into her night clothes and joins us for popcorn and television until we're all too tired to see straight.

This is how things should be, I think as I drag myself to bed. Mom, Jazz and me. All together and laughing and smiling. It hasn't been that way for so long. Not because we don't love each other, but because we're all so focused on our own thing. Mom on work in order to support us. Me on keeping under the radar. Jazz trying to...not be like me, I guess. All this is sad because this is a time in our lives where we could use each other the most and we're all running in opposite directions and tripping over our own feet.

I only wish I knew how to fix it.

7

Diary of a Noble

I am a hooker.

Or, at least, I'll be one on stage. I'm terrified out of my mind, but if M thinks I can do it...I want to prove her right.

I wonder if baby sister will come to the play. She used to love to watch me act and would help me practice my lines. I'd be lying if I said I wasn't at least partially willing to do this in hopes of making her proud. Will she point at me on stage and say, "That's my sister"? Or will she hide in the back row and keep her eyes on her phone the whole time?

Man, I sound pathetic. I just really miss my family.

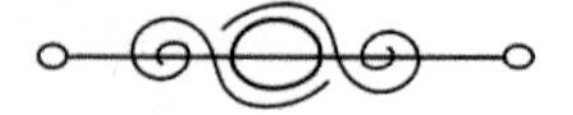

Wade and Trevor are absent from Drama the next two days due to swim practice. Not typically a winter sport for most schools, but Maple Burrow happens to be blessed with the fanciest of technology that is so clearly impertinent to our learning environment. Like an indoor heated pool. My middle school had a pool. Outdoors. Which meant we were lucky if we had two weeks out of the year wherein it was both clean enough and warm enough to swim during gym class.

Even with only Amber, Mara, and me in our group we manage to get a good chunk done on the sets and I show them some of the design sketches I've drawn up for Mara's costume. She fusses over how wonderful it is until my face is so hot I'm sure it's going to have a nuclear meltdown.

Come to think of it, with Wade not in drama I don't think I've said more than a passing hello to him in a number of days. Not until I'm leaving school on Friday and I get a text from a number I don't recognize. *Plans tonight?*

There isn't a number in my phone that doesn't belong to a family member. Last year, I forced myself to purge my contact list of the few people from middle school who disowned me. So it's very likely this is a wrong number.

Who is this? I write back.

Wade.

Oh. Unexpected. Not bad, though Jazz will have a hernia if she gets in the car and finds me texting her dream guy. Assuming she didn't already leave to catch a bus across town to Dad's. *No plans. Why?*

By the time he writes back, I've also gotten a text from Jazz confirming my suspicions. At least her wording is nice. Not as clipped and cold as it has been. See what happens when she takes her medicine as directed?

Wade responds: *Finished the script. Wanted your opinion?*

That isn't really a question, but I won't whine about grammar over text. I consider this. It's Friday. He had all day to show me the script but hadn't said a word about it. Why he wants me to be the first to read, then, I have no idea. It means he wants to spend time with me outside of school and I cannot recall the last time I hung out with anyone from school off of school property. Of course, this could be his roundabout way of getting me alone to "talk." Which means it should be somewhere private.

Jazz will be gone. Mom is working, as per usual, so— *My place @ 6?*

Wade says that works for him. I give him the address and jokingly say he better show up with food if I'm going to be missing dinner to read his script.

So when he shows up at six on the dot with a pizza and a two liter of soda, I can't help but laugh. "What if I'm allergic to cheese?"

His expression sobers and he looks at the box, frowning deeply. "Are you?"

"No, you adorable dork. Get in here." I let him in out of the cold, trying not to be self-conscious as he takes a seat in our small living room and looks around. I don't know what his house looks like, but given his name brand clothes and nearly new truck, I'm willing to bet this apartment is the size of his garage. Whether he's thinking any of that or not, he doesn't say. Perfectly polite gentleman.

I fetch paper plates and some napkins and plop onto the other side of the couch. I tell Wade he didn't actually have to get me food, but he shrugs and says he was hungry, too. We're quiet as we eat.

When he's done, which is before I am, he pulls the script from his backpack and places it on the cushion between us. Geez, did he actually come here just to have me read it? I cram the rest of the crust into my mouth, dust my hands off, and flip through until I find the last page I remember reading on my copy. Skimming, mostly. Not that it's a long play, but it's long enough that I'm going to tear my hair out memorizing Mable's snappy lines.

Wade sips his glass of soda and watches nothing in particular on the wall. Like he's waiting. For...a reaction? Comments? Criticism?

ANNA

It was you all along! My husband has been in your bed!

MABLE

He says it's more accommodating than yours. Can you blame him? Maybe you just don't know what you're missing out on.

Anna is indignant. Mable grabs her face in her hands and lays a kiss on her mouth.

I jerk my hand from the papers like they've caught fire. "I'm supposed to *kiss Mara?*"

Wade stares down at his hands. "It's a rough draft. I can make changes, if you want."

My mouth opens and closes uselessly. He still won't look my way. "Are you... Did you include this in here *for* me?"

Finally he twists to level a look in my direction. "It's the only way you're going to get to kiss her."

The statement wasn't meant to be mean, but it hurts all the same. It must show in my face because Wade drops his gaze and stares into his soda.

"I didn't mean like..."

"No, no. You're completely right. Mara's straight and obviously taken." I swallow back the lump in my throat. "That's not the point. I don't know if—doesn't it seem like I'd be taking advantage of her?"

"It's part of the play, London," Wade says patiently. "You can't tell me you think it's out of character for Mable.

"No, I guess not."

On some level, I'm touched. Wade did this, wrote this in, for *me*. Knowing the others might give him grief about it. He was trying to do me a favor.

"If our situations were reversed... Would you do it?" I ask.

One of Wade's eyebrows twitches up. "Kiss Mara? No."

I shove at his arm. "Not what I meant. If you had the chance to lock lips with some guy you really had a thing for?"

"It's different for guys." He shifts in his seat like he can't get comfortable, like the words have to be forced out of his throat through a grater. "It's cool if two chicks are comfortable enough with their sexuality to do something like that on stage. People will laugh. But two guys? Nuh-uh."

There is truth in what he says. Seeing two girls kissing—play or not—will have mixed reactions amongst our audience as long as they think it's acting. Two guys doing it, though...I don't even want to think about it. It's a shitty double-standard. Lesbians can be ignored. Gay guys are sent to the darkest pits of hell.

I return to the script to read a little further on. Stepping back and looking at it from a spectator's view, it is a great scene and is actually tasteful and serves a purpose. Very Rocky Horroresque in its upbeat, fast-paced dialogue and exaggerated body language. I wonder what Mara will think when she reads it. Thankfully no singing and dancing.

"Do your parents know?" Wade asks.

"About me being in the play...?"

"About you wanting in Mara's pants."

I look up, expression flat. "About me being gay, you mean? No. I don't talk to my dad anyway, but even if I did..." Where did that question come from? Unless it's one of those things where he's trying to broach the subject but doesn't know how. "What about yours?"

His face blanches at the mere mention of it. "God, no."

"They wouldn't take it well, huh?"

"I have two older brothers and parents who are all very particular about appearance and image," he says solemnly. "If I told them, I'm not so sure I would have a place to live anymore."

I stare at the downward turn of his mouth, unable to imagine that. If my family found out? Sure, they probably wouldn't be happy. Jazz would never let me hear the end of it. But I'd never be *thrown out* onto the street. I wouldn't be disowned. It strikes me how lucky I am in that moment to have a mother who would love me regardless of who I loved.

"They might just need time to get used to it," I offer, at a loss for what else to say. "That happens. Taking time to adjust or something."

"You don't know my family." He sounds tired, like he's thought of this a hundred times before, turned it over in his head until it hurts, trying to think of a way to make it work. He's quick to add, "I don't even know if I am for sure. It's not like I've really..."

"What, had sex with a guy?" I snort. "I haven't had sex with a girl. It's not about that."

That I've put it so crudely into words makes Wade's face do funny things. For half a second I'm worried I've scared him away from the topic. "Right. What's it about, then?"

"It's about loving who you love. Being attracted to who you're attracted to." Shrug. "I don't actually have anything against guys. I can find them attractive."

Wade squints like he doesn't believe me. "You do?"

"On some level, yeah. Probably like how straight girls look at other girls. For instance, I think you're a hottie." I grin at the awkward twist of his expression. "It doesn't mean I want to throw you on the floor and have my way with you."

"But you've wanted to. With girls, I mean. When did that start?"

That's something I've thought about a lot over the years, and something I can pinpoint easily. "In seventh grade I had these two friends, Delaine and Lisa. Sisters. We spent all our free time together." I close my eyes, still able to picture their faces, clear as day. Lisa was cynical and dry-humored. Delaine was bubbly and laughed a lot, and she was so smart. There wasn't a topic she didn't know something about. "It was little stuff at first. Girls are affectionate with each other, you know? Holding arms and cuddling or whatever. I started getting butterflies in my stomach whenever Delaine would look at me or touch me, like I couldn't figure out how to talk anymore. I didn't understand it until much later. Way after we weren't talking anymore."

When I open my eyes, Wade is watching me so enrapt that it makes me blush. He asks, "What happened with her?"

I shake my head. "We went to different high schools. We dropped out of touch. Out of sight, out of mind." I don't say it was a decision on Delaine's part after I admitted to her that I liked girls. The look on her face as she undoubtedly thought about all the times we'd shared a room, shared a *bed*, shared space while changing clothes. For months, I called and e-mailed trying to make plans. Eventually it got exhausting—and painful—to try anymore. But to tell all this to Wade seems like a bad idea when I'm trying to encourage him it's okay. "Your turn. What made you suspect it?"

Wade opens his mouth, closes it again, runs a hand over his shaved head and averts his eyes. I give him as long as he needs. Which unfortunately is too long because just when I think he's going to spill the details, the front door swings open and Mom shuffles in out of the rain, shoes sloshing and umbrella dangling from her arm.

"Whoo-ee, brr, who gave winter permission to start?" She turns toward the living room and her spine stiffens as her eyes widen in surprise. Maybe not so much that we have company, but that *I* have company. Me. The antisocial one. The one who has never had a boyfriend...has a *boy* in the house. Alone.

I am not helping matters by looking guilty for some reason and blurting out, "You're home early."

"Obviously." Mom blinks, hanging the umbrella from the coat hook by the door.

Wade, bless his face, gets to his feet and steps over, offering a hand out to Mom. "Nice to meet you, Ms. Noble. I'm Wade Jones."

Score one for Wade. Mom is a sucker for politeness. She takes his hand and her mouth pulls up into an amiable U. "Just Kathy is fine. Nice to meet you, Wade. Sorry, if I'd known London was having company I would've brought dinner home for you both."

Wade gives her hand a shake and draws back. "Oh, nah. I took care of it. We have plenty of pizza if you'd like some."

As he turns to retrieve the pizza box from the coffee table, Mom leans to one side to give me a little *O* face. She points at Wade and mouths *he bought you dinner?* I give her a look consisting of raised eyebrows and a flick of my hand that clearly says *for the love of God, please don't embarrass me.*

"I'm famished," Mom says when Wade offers her the box. "I'll just...uh. Take this in the kitchen. I have a few calls to make, so you two just..." She waves at nothing in particular with a silly little smile. "Have fun. Do your thing."

"I should actually be getting home." Wade's smile is shy and faint, but I think it's genuine. I don't see him sincerely smile often; it's nice.

"So soon?" Mom catches the impatient roll of my eyes from over Wade's shoulder and she inches back for the kitchen. "Well, that's a shame. It was lovely to meet you, Wade. Thank you for the dinner~ Give me some warning next time and I'll cook for everyone." Then she disappears around the corner.

I heave a sigh. "You don't want her cooking."

Wade turns that halfway smile to me. He thanks me for having him over and says that my mom is nice and that I look like her, which I think I'll take as a compliment because guys are always hitting on Mom when we're out. He leaves me with the updated script copy, and it's a reminder that I never did tell him if I wanted that kiss with Mable and Anna to stay as it was or not. Guess it gives me a few days to think about it.

As soon as Wade has left, I pop into the kitchen. Mom is chowing down on the last of the pizza like she hasn't eaten all day. She probably hasn't. Morning and afternoon would have been spent at Amelia Crippley's, the elderly woman she helps look after a few days a week. From there, she would have gone straight to the diner for the evening shift. Between both jobs, Mom is lucky to have a full twenty-four hours off maybe once a month.

She greets me with a smile and a smear of tomato sauce on the corner of her mouth that she licks away a second later. "You didn't tell me you had a boyfriend."

"Woah, *not* a boyfriend. At all." I hold up my hands and try not to feel a little pang of regret at the disappointment on Mom's face. Guess she'd be happy if I hooked up with some guy, even if she'd then have to give me this long speech about safe sex and waiting for the *right one*. "He's a friend. Not even a good friend because it's a new thing."

"Hm." Mom picks off a pepperoni and eats it solo. "Where'd you meet him?"

"Drama." And when she looks confused, I add: "After-school. I joined the club last week."

Mom stops in mid-bite and lowers her slice, eyes all wide and shining. "You joined a club? You didn't tell me that."

"You were busy. I've hardly seen you."

Her smile dims and she turns away. I grimace. Mom's feelings are a delicate thing. She's a nice woman, friendly and polite, but she takes things really personal and carries a lot on her shoulders because she thinks everything is somehow a failing on her part. Which, more often than not, makes me feel like these things are *my* fault because she shouldn't have to worry about me so much.

"I'm sorry, babe." Mom rinses her hands and dries them on a dish towel. "I know I've been absent a lot lately. I promise, after the holidays..."

"You really don't have to justify it to me." Once upon a time, she did. When I was younger and didn't understand. I was mad at her, mad at Dad, mad at myself. Given that I'm eighteen and the prospect of getting my own place, college, and a job are looming in my not-so-distant future, the concept of money and how damned necessary it is has made me a little more aware of what Mom goes through.

She is silent for a moment and I stare at the back of her head and the wayward strands of hair sticking out from her hair clip. She takes a deep breath before turning back to me, her smile in place once more. "Does this mean you'll be in plays again? I always loved seeing you act."

My stomach twists. Mom, watching me playing a whore? How awesome is that going to be? I won't point out that I was only in a handful of real plays and Mom was only ever able to watch them recorded later. Work kept her from attending in person. Still... "I hope so. I'll let you know."

Diary of a Noble

It feels immoral. Immoral? Is that the word I'm looking for? It sounded better than 'it feels wrong,' even though it does. Getting to kiss M? Awesome. Getting to kiss M only because it's written in the script and she's too dedicated to her craft to say no? Not so awesome.

I guess I should tell W to change it. Maybe.

8

Wade finishes the script halfway through the week. I find everyone reading it Wednesday afternoon and I pretend like I haven't already seen most of it as I take a seat and go through it again. Slowly. Hoping Mara will get to our kiss before I do so I can see her reaction and act accordingly. She finishes the entire thing with no commentary in the middle. "Wade, this is so awesome. Our performance is going to blow everyone else out of the water."

I realize I've been biting the hell out of my lower lip. Something that doesn't stop until I'm convinced Mara isn't going to shriek about how kissing another girl is way too gross. Maybe she's simply the sort who can differentiate between reality and the character she's playing. I only hope I can do the same.

Mara grabs Trevor's arm and drags him across the theater to run lines. Wade casts me a thin smile. "You're welcome."

My face burns. I still have no clue if this is a good idea or a really bad one. I flip Wade off and he shrugs and wanders after Mara and Trevor to watch and give direction, since he's our director on top of our script-writer. Which leaves me and Amber alone.

She flips her script shut and nudges her glasses up the bridge of her nose. "What was that about?"

"Hm?" I busy myself re-reading some of my lines. I'm going to need practice, too. Lots of it. I'm in fewer scenes than the others, but I'm pretty sure I have the longest lines.

Amber studies me. "Nevermind. You want to help me with the sets?"

Shrugging, I get to my feet to follow Amber to the back of the stage. Most people have abandoned their props today because scripts were supposed to be done, which means everyone is talking and rehearsing and fine-tuning so it's just me and Amber and a group of boys at the opposite end of the stage painting balloons on a blue sky.

Amber gets me painting—with direction, of course—and I find myself chewing at my lip again. "What do you think of the script?"

She shrugs. "I'm not in the play. Should I have an opinion on it?"

"I don't see why not." I glance at her. "You don't think the teachers are going to throw a fit or anything, do you?"

"It's not like you guys will be stripping off your clothes or anything." Amber sighs, nudges her glasses again, and leans in close to work on the detailed veining of some leaves. She's good at this. Really good. I look at the blob of blue that is supposed to be a curtain beneath my own brush. Yuck.

"No, but...there's kissing. Like, a lot of it."

"Not that much."

"Hm." Not helpful. "How come you don't like to act?"

Amber pauses. Just for a second. Like the question catches her off-guard. "Why would I?"

"I don't know. It's fun pretending to be someone else."

"In front of all those people? Way more attention and eyes on me than I would like."

That earns her a curious look from me, though her head is down and she's painting again. She's self-conscious, I'm gathering, which I think is sad. She's curvy in a really nice way and she has a pretty face. I think people overlook her because she makes it a point to pull her hair back, keep her head down, and wear the most non-descript version of our uniform as she possibly can. She's a blender. She blends, so she isn't noticed.

Including by me. I've never noticed her before, either, despite that we've shared a class or two over the years. Also sad because maybe that means we have more in common than I originally thought.

"Do you want to go out sometime?" I blurt.

Amber rocks back onto the balls of her feet, elbows on her knees, mouth drawn thin. "Why would you ask me that?"

Or maybe I'm misreading her entirely and she just doesn't like me. Maybe she actually has a big group of friends that simply aren't interested in drama, and she doesn't want to act because she prefers being behind the scenes.

Still, I meet her eyes and force my lips into a weird smile. "I don't get out much. Sorry. I'm really bad at this whole making plans thing." Especially when I didn't have time to prepare for it. I hadn't geared up for asking anyone to do anything. I've kind of burned myself out on being sociable by hanging out with Wade.

Amber hmm's. She hunches over, her blonde ponytail sliding forward over her shoulder. "Yeah, sure, I guess so."

"Yeah?" That wasn't so hard. Awkward maybe, but not hard. "Cool."

We don't talk about it. We don't discuss what we'll do or how much fun it'll be or anything like I've heard Jazz do with her friends. Amber and I continue to work in complete silence and I can only hope when we hang out together, it isn't like this.

Before we leave, we make tentative plans for her to pick me up at six on Saturday. Wade walks me to the parking lot and I tell him I have plans. Like, real plans. With someone who maybe can be a friend. "I mean, people don't go out with other people unless they at least want to try being friends, right?"

He shrugs. "I guess so."

I sigh. "I don't know why I'm asking you. You always seem to have plans with someone or another."

"Beats being at home."

It's a weird admission. One that gets me to peer at him in hopes of him elaborating, but he doesn't.

Jazz is waiting around outside on her phone, her head down. I'm surprised she didn't take off with one of her friends or bus it home.

"God," she says without looking up. "Took you long enough."

"Hi Jasmine," Wade greets.

Jazz does a double take and nearly sends her phone crash-landing on the pavement in her hurry to straighten up, push the hair from her face, adjust her skirt, and look sweet all at once. She hasn't let me live it down ever since she found out Wade came over. A lot of shrieking and *how could you?* ensued.

"Wade! Hey." Her voice drips saccharine. "You look nice today. How are you?"

He gives her a peculiar look, a tilt of his head. It's the look I've noticed he gives all girls who make eyes at him. Like he's flattered but really has no idea what to do with the attention. "Thanks. I'm good. Just talking with your sister."

The way he says it makes me wonder if he does that on purpose. Mentions me and her being sisters. It makes me smile. "Yep. So I'll see you tomorrow."

Wade gives me a nod, shoves his hands in his pockets and wanders off to his truck. Jazz wiggles her fingers after him, smile firmly in place even as she says to me through grit teeth, "What is going on between you two?"

I laugh and get in the car. If only she knew how funny that question is. Jazz scurries to the other side and throws herself into the passenger's seat.

"What's that laugh supposed to mean?"

"What do you want me to say, Jazz? We've been screwing around in the bathrooms between classes?" I start the car. "Unlike some girls, I'm perfectly capable of having a guy friend without there being something romantic involved."

She huffs and folds her arms, staring out the window with all the maturity of a five-year-old. "Are you at least putting in a good word for me?"

"I tell him the truth, if that's what you mean."

She groans.

9

Diary of a Noble

I'm starting to build a better picture of the kind of family W has. He's a straight-A student, polite to all the teachers, doesn't talk much even when he's around 'the guys.' M and I went to watch him and T at swim practice one day and even when in the groove of doing laps he's very no-nonsense and straight-faced. The guy doesn't know how to relax.

I can only assume it's a family thing. Parents who push for perfection. Here's hoping he's not the sort of person who internalizes everything and gets pushed and pushed and pushed, until he snaps and shoots up the school or himself.

I hope he'll talk to me more. It makes me feel better. I like to think it makes him feel better, too.

10

The rest of the week is spent alternating between helping Amber with sets and running lines. So far none of them with Mara, always with Trevor. I must be doing a decent job because Wade doesn't correct me. Not like he does with Trevor, who is definitely not an actor by nature. He reads his lines stiffly and stumbles over his words now and again, but he's getting better.

Amber and I don't talk much. When I say we don't talk 'much,' I mean we talk more than we did my first week here but not as frequently or in-depth as most people do. I talk to Mara, though. Every time Mara pays me any sort of attention I can't help but fall all over myself. I really hope I'm not trying too hard to be interesting or funny or smart and having the opposite effect of appealing to her. I don't know what the point in trying so hard is. It's not like she would be interested anyway, but I guess I can't stand the idea of her not liking me.

Thursday she says she hears I'm hanging out with Amber this weekend. She could've only heard this from Wade or from Amber herself. Either way, it's bizarre to think of anyone talking about me when I'm not there. So I shrug and say yeah, even though I have no idea where we're going or what we're doing.

Then Mara draws her script toward her face, peering at me over the top of it so all I can see are her deep brown eyes and the smooth arches of her brows, and she asks, "Do you want to hang out sometime?"

By some miracle, I manage not to stutter and my head doesn't explode and I don't swallow my own tongue. "I'd really like that," I say, and grin to show her just how much I mean it.

Mara leans forward. "I was sort of thinking, maybe sometime...we should go on a double date."

Any thoughts that had floated into my head of spending one-on-one time with Mara dissipate. Watching a movie together, shopping, playing video games. (Does she even like video games? I don't actually know what she does in her spare time. She doesn't talk much about it.)

"A double date," I repeat, perplexed.

"Me and Trevor." She glances over her shoulder at the boys. "With you and Wade, maybe?"

I open my mouth, at a loss for words. "Wade and I aren't a couple."

"Oh, no! I know. But I think he likes you, you know?" She squints, tipping her head in this cutely thoughtful way she does when trying to explain something she finds complex. "He never spends any time with other girls, yet he actually went over to your house and was excited to have you in the group. I mean, that's really big for Wade."

I draw my bottom lip between my teeth. No, no, no. She has it all so wrong. Can I blame her? From an outsider's perspective, I can kinda see it. Wade and I have been hanging out a bit. He stops in the halls to talk to me at my locker. Yesterday I dropped by him and his friends at lunch to give him some brownies I had made, because he told me he had a thing for marshmallow brownies. None of it is anything I wouldn't have done for any friend. It's just that I don't really have other friends for her to make a comparison to.

Is Wade a friend now? I like to think he is. We know each other's biggest secret. If that doesn't speak friendship I don't know what does. Explaining that to Mara without giving anything away, though... "I think you might have the wrong idea. Wade and I click really well as friends, but—"

Mara is having none of it. She's already talking about how Wade is a great guy, how nice he is, how thoughtful. I'm agreeing with her—because it is all true—and it only digs my grave deeper. Before I've left for the day, it would seem I've been set up...on a double date. What is Wade going to say about that? No, forget Wade. What is *Jazz* going to say?

11

Wade arrives at my door fifteen minutes early on Friday night, while I'm still trying to decide what to wear. Words cannot express how grateful I am he chose to pick me up alone rather than with Mara and Trevor in tow. I can handle one person in my house. I'm not so sure about three.

"You seem like the type who would have pets," Wade comments, trailing after me into the room I share with Jazz who is, thankfully, in the shower. I hope to be dressed and out of here by the time she's done so she doesn't ask questions. I didn't tell her where I'm going, just that I'm going *out.*

"No pets," I say, rifling through my side of the closet. "We had a dog growing up but we had to put him down a few years ago. He was old."

Wade says "Oh," and sits on the edge of my bed, examining the posters and pictures on the walls. "Sorry."

"I'd love to have another one. Don't really have the time for it." More like, pet food and the proper veterinary care would cost more than we can afford. I can't bring myself to say that to someone who probably doesn't even think about that sort of thing. If he wanted a dog, I bet he could go out and buy one. And I don't want to give him the impression we're dirt poor. We're not. We're just...careful spenders because crises have a tendency of popping up for our family. Car problems, medical emergencies, school expenses and so forth.

"Is this you?"

I twist around, jeans and a band t-shirt in hand. Safe enough for going out, I hope. Wade is pointing at a photo of Delaine, Lisa, and myself from our eighth grade graduation. In it, I'm dressed in jewelry and pink and orange and my hair is platinum blonde with pink peekaboos in my bangs. It's the 'old London' so no wonder it must seem like a complete stranger to Wade.

"That's me," I agree, voice tight, and turn away to start getting changed.

I used to have the most eclectic wardrobe, with rainbows and unicorns and bright colors everywhere. I kept my hair spiked and dyed weird colors. Mom let me even though I was only in middle school because she thought it was important Jasmine and I always have freedom over our bodies and identities.

I still keep my hair pretty short, but it lays flat and it's my natural, darker blonde. I haven't worn anything to school besides the required uniform—even on casual Fridays—in three years. What was the point of blending in if I was going to ruin it by dressing so bizarrely once a week?

"It's a nice look. All the colors." He glances at me. I make a twirling motion and Wade rolls his eyes and turns around. In a sense, I guess getting changed in front of a gay guy isn't any different than getting changed in front of girls in gym. Is that how it works? It's not like he'd be checking me out. "I don't think I've ever seen you in anything but the uniform, actually."

"Yeah, I don't know," is my awkward response because I *don't* know. How to answer that, that is. Not without explaining more about me than I'd care to.

Wade shrugs and drops the subject. We leave before Jazz can get out of the shower and freak out about the fact I had Wade in our room, on my bed, while I was getting changed.

Wade offers to do the driving and I won't complain; my car isn't the most amazing contraption on the planet, especially when compared with his hybrid that still smells like it just came off the lot. Not every kid at Mapple Burrow has their own parent-provided car, but enough do that make it the norm. Honestly, the only reason I have one is because although it was Dad's, the title was in Mom's name and she wasn't letting him keep it after all the debt he left her with. So—voila. Car for me. Technically, for me and Jazz both, but she doesn't have a license yet.

I sink into the passenger's seat and enjoy the wonders of heated seats and Wade's mp3 player hooked up to the stereo. It's cozy and warm and he surprises me by having pretty awesome music taste. Wade tells me where we're meeting up with Mara and Trevor. Some diner called Rosie's Kitchen a few blocks from the theater so we can grab a bite before catching a movie. I tip my head back and tap my feet against the floorboards.

"This doesn't strike you as totally bizarre and uncomfortable?"

Wade shrugs. "I don't know. It's just an outing. Not thinking much of it."

"You realize Mara's hell bent on hooking us up."

"Yeah. So?"

"So...we're sort of incompatible."

Wade purses his lips, searching for a parking spot. "If it gets people off our backs for a little while, I don't see what the big deal is. Did you have something else planned tonight?"

The comment stings a bit. I cross my arms and stare straight ahead.

He pulls into a parallel spot with ease and sighs. "I didn't mean it like that."

"Yes you did, but it's fine." I shrug, distracted now by the scenery outside.

Wade gets out of the car and circles around. He leans over, peering at me through the window. "Coming?"

My throat is dry. I try to tell myself tonight won't be as big of a disaster as I'm worried it will be.

We take a seat in a booth near the far corner, away from the door and the chill it lets in, but next to the window because I enjoy people-watching and the rain outside is pretty. Rain is always nice, so long as I'm not stuck out in it. Wade sits beside me and it feels weird having someone in my space, but Trevor and Mara will be sitting across from us so I guess it's only natural. This is double-date seating. We barely have time to look at our menus before our fellow couple spots us.

Mara is all bright smiles and wide, pretty eyes. Raindrops dot her lashes and hair and make her look like some sort of Christmas doll. I want to hold her face in my hands and stare at her awhile. That would probably be weird. Especially with her boyfriend present.

"I've never eaten here," Mara says after typical greetings are exchanged. She drapes her wet coat over the back of her booth seat.

Trevor mutters, "What a dump," and Mara elbows him sharply.

"I think it's cozy. Doesn't hurt to try something new once in awhile."

With the looks they exchange, I feel as though I've missed a vital part of the conversation. It occurred to me in the car that this really doesn't strike me as the sort of place they would come to. It isn't fancy or expensive or up-scale, even as far as diners go. This is more on par with Bruno's. I know most of the places the rich kids hang out, and this? This isn't it.

I don't say anything, though. I just stare down at the menu on the paper placemats and try to decide what I want to eat that won't cost me all my pocket money. Money that Mom was more than happy to give me when I told her I was going out with friends, but money I felt guilty for taking.

Over dinner, we talk about school. And drama. And the play. Because it's safe territory and I don't have to worry about anything coming up that I don't want to discuss. Mara talks about how she wants to get into a real acting school when she graduates and how she's already been in a few commercials—only local—but she feels she can make it big. I don't doubt it. She has the personality. I say, "I'd go see any movie you were in," and she blushes and laughs, smacking my arm lightly.

She goes on to say Trevor wants to get into the computer industry. Not just programming, but designing new processors and chips and hardware. I'll admit, looking at Trevor with his preppy face and toned body, you wouldn't expect that out of him.

I nudge Wade and ask, "What're you going to college for, then?"

Wade chews absently at one of his fries, but doesn't look at me. "Medical degree, I guess. Or law."

My nose wrinkles. "How cliché. Also unexpected, coming from you."

Trevor laughs. "His old man doesn't give him much of a choice. Not if he wants them to pay for his tuition." That earns him a sour look from across the table and Trevor shrugs. "What? Man, it's not like I'm in any better shape. My mom's convinced computers are going to be running and building themselves ten years from now and getting into the business is pointless. I've got to secure a scholarship if I want to go anywhere."

I watch Wade from the corner of my eye. I'm starting to get a better picture of these parents of his. Overbearing. Pushy. 'My way or the highway.' I'm also starting to think Wade is doing exactly what I'm doing: keeping his head down and trying to ride out the storm until he can be left to his own devices.

"If it were your choice," I ask Wade, "what would you go to college for?"

He lowers the cup he had to his mouth and studies me. His expressions are always so damn unreadable, but there's a faint crinkle between his brows, like no one has ever asked him that. Like he's said, 'my parents want me to do this' and everyone in the world has accepted it. Including him.

"Religious studies," he says.

"Really?" Mara steals one of Trevor's fries. "Like...what do you do with that? I mean, what kind of jobs?"

Wade shrugs. Shutting down again because he's uncomfortable. Or maybe he honestly doesn't know himself. His silence is painful to watch.

"Teaching," I offer.

Trevor chortles. "Taking a class just to teach it always seemed weird to me."

I glare. "He could be a historian. A researcher. He could publish a book, or write thesis papers. There's plenty you can do with that kind of degree. *I* think it's interesting."

"Sure." Trevor looks amused while I'm resisting the urge to reach across the table and pop him in the mouth for not being more supportive of his best friend. "Okay then, London, what are you going to college for?"

All eyes are on me. I just stare, trapped. I haven't given after-high school much thought. If I'm able to manage college, it'll be the community college where I can work part time and pay my tuition while I'm at it. Nothing impressive. Nothing interesting.

"I haven't decided."

"Design?" offers Wade.

Mara brightens. "Oh, that would be perfect for her, huh? Like, designing costumes and stuff."

"I don't think I'm good enough for that," I say, dropping my gaze to my food.

"If everyone were good at what they do naturally, then what point would there be to college?" Trevor drawls. Guess he has a point.

I dip one of my chicken strips into its sauce thoughtfully, like the task in of itself is an art. "What about...like, a makeup artist? Not just regular makeup, but stage makeup."

Wade snaps. "Masks? Special effects? For all those horror movies."

I snap right back at him, grinning. "Exactly. Wouldn't that be cool? I did Jazz's Halloween makeup every year growing up. I wasn't half bad."

"Mara will be the actress and you can be her makeup artist," Trevor says.

We share a laugh over that. We eat our food and we talk and we smile until our faces ache, and I think this is the first time since Delaine and Lisa that I've been able to be this happy. Like I have friends. Friends who think I matter. Who care about my future and believe I'm good at something.

The movie almost seems like the downturn of our night because it means less talking. Even though we just ate, Wade gets us popcorn to split, and drinks, and he ignores me when I try to give him my cash when the others aren't paying attention. He already paid for my dinner and since this isn't supposed to *really* be a date between us...

"Forget it," he murmurs, pushing my hand away. "Just let me get it. Bring me more of those brownies or something and we'll call it even."

I shove the cash into my pocket, moping. I had to suck it up and go to Mom for this money, and now it's not even getting put to use. The movie is some sort of sci-fi action thing that Mara wrinkles her nose at, but I think looks cool, and the boys will enjoy just because shit gets blown up a lot. Even in the (relative) silence of the theater, I'm enjoying their company.

Even if I have no fucking clue what to do when Wade reaches out and takes my hand.

In retrospect, maybe I should have pulled away. Or maybe I should've leaned over and asked him what he was doing. It would have been the natural progression of a date, something that anyone else would be ecstatic for. The cute guy they're seeing a movie with slips his hand around hers, fingers intertwining. Their eyes meet. Sparks fly. Romance and magic and baby-making ensues.

Except when Wade took my hand all I did was stare at it, bewildered, not understanding why it was there.

I don't ask him. Mainly because I can't think of a nice way to say *why were you touching me?* On the car ride home I keep my hands tucked under my arms so he can't do it again. Which might be mean, but not as mean as pulling away or something, right?

Wade turns onto my street. He has the frown of the century on his face so I ask, "What's eating you?"

"Nothing." He stops outside my apartment building but he's lingering, like he has something to say. I give him a minute because I'm coming to learn that sometimes all Wade needs is a minute or two for his words to make it past the internal filter in his brain. Not a filter like some people have. Not a filter that scans for *is this appropriate/will it hurt their feelings/am I swearing in front of my mother*? His filter is more like *am I going to be rejected or ridiculed if I say this thing?*

So I wait. Eventually Wade is able to say, "Will you be my girlfriend?"

Silence.

What the hell?

I stare at him through the darkness. "I know you like to dance around the subject and avoid stating the blatantly obvious, but...you *do* realize I'm a lesbian."

Wade keeps his head turned straight. The dashboard lights cast a gloomy glow on his grim mouth. I really wish he would smile more. "Yes."

"And you're gay."

He frowns.

"So why...?"

Wade breathes in, out again, then twists in his seat to face me. "You had fun tonight."

"Well, yeah, sure. It was a good time."

"Mara had fun. Trevor had fun. If we keep going out as a group, people will start talking. If we're hanging out and going on double dates, isn't it going to look really weird if we aren't actually dating?"

His logic makes sense...I guess? "But..."

"I like you, London."

"I like you, too."

He reaches out for my hand. I let him. "We could both benefit from this, don't you see? We want to get through our last year of high school. We get along. I enjoy being around you. You have this...way of talking to people that makes them feel good about themselves. You never talk down to anyone."

I look at our joined hands. "So we'd be fake-dating. Basically just friends doing friend-stuff but calling it dating because we're a guy and a girl and that's what's expected of us."

Wade drops his gaze, worry lining his features. "You make it sound like a bad thing."

"I don't honestly know." I worry at the inside of my lip. "What about some other girl? What about Jazz? She's hot for you and she'd jump at the chance."

"That's the problem," Wade says solemnly. "I can't date someone that *actually* has feelings for me. I don't want to hurt them."

"She'll murder me. She'll smother me with a pillow in my sleep." My fingers curl. His palms are clammy. This conversation is taking everything out of him and I feel the weight of this decision pressing in on me from every side.

"It's no less consideration than she's shown you," he says.

True. Jazz hasn't done anything relating to our school life that has accommodated me. Nothing to make me feel better. Nothing to help me cope. Whereas I've kept out of her way and done everything I can to avoid letting her friends even know my name.

In all honesty, I'm really sick of it. It's one thing for me to hide who I am because of my own choices but to do it because someone else would be ashamed? It's not fair. I can't deny that the last few weeks since joining drama, hanging out with Mara, Wade, Trevor, and Amber, I've had more fun than the last three and a half years combined. I might have a shot at having a real social life again.

All I have to do is compromise myself a little longer, I guess. Really, is it any different than what I've been doing? If these people became my friends, my real, true, honest friends, could I tell them? That I'm gay, and how my sister pretends I don't exist day after day breaks my heart? Or that my dad was in rehab and even as I'm hating him I miss him so much it hurts? Can I really start chipping off this lackluster shell and be *me* again? So many questions I don't have time to think out answers to.

"I'm not going to tell people we're dating. But if you really want, I won't deny it either."

Wade's shoulders relax. I doubt it's exactly the answer he wanted, but the way he squeezes my hand suggests that it's enough.

I have a sort-of-not-boyfriend. I'm sure I'm not the first lesbian with this problem. This bothers me and I think it's going to help Wade a lot more than it's going to help me. He has a family to keep up appearances with and people at school constantly hounding him. Me? I'm a nobody. Letting anyone run with the assumption that we're together is not going to benefit me in any way.

Jasmine happens to be waiting up in the living room, still dressed and done up, probably anticipating Wade coming in with me.

"Look who's back," she comments idly. Nonchalant. "Where'd you guys go?"

I'm feeling spiteful. Wade picked open a raw wound bringing up Jazz's treatment of me at school, and the fact that now all my new friends are aware of how embarrassed she is of me. I lean against the wall while I pull off my shoes. "Oh, you know. We skipped out on dinner and a movie to have sex in the back of his car all night."

Jazz's eyes nearly pop out of her head. Sadly, it doesn't actually make me feel any better. "That's not funny. You guys aren't even a couple."

"Hm."

She squints, trying to make heads or tails of my expression. "You aren't. Are you?"

I shrug. Noncommittal. Not admitting but not denying, either. I straighten up and cross my arms, refusing to let her see that I'm inwardly wincing at having to leave this out in the open when I could so easily say *there's nothing going on.* She's never been considerate of my feelings. Why should I care about hers?

Jasmine sizes me up and when she seems to determine I am now her least favorite person in the world because my lack of denying my guilt must mean that I am, in fact, jumping Wade in the back of his car, she looks away, returning her attention to the television. A pang of guilt makes me take a step toward her.

"Jazz..."

"Shut up." Her wavering voice betrays her stoic expression. "I'm watching something."

I am the world's worst sister. Maybe the worst person in general. Not only was I expecting that crushing her pretty princess feelings would make me feel better, but I had *hoped* it would.

I don't feel better. I feel like dirt.

12

Diary of a Noble

What the hell have I gotten myself into?

Thank God it's Saturday. Wade texts to ask if I told Jazz and how she took it and I reply, *we'll find out if I'm still alive come Monday.* These thoughts and problems have me so wrapped up in myself that I totally spaced the fact that I have another play-date today. Amber calls to ask if we're still on for this afternoon. I'm really not feeling up for company, but I was the one who asked her to hang out and I'm not going to ditch her because I'm feeling like a bad person.

Jazz stormed out of the apartment pretty early this morning. I'm not even sure she slept in the room; she was on the couch when I went to bed, and she was doing her makeup in the bathroom when I woke up. She doesn't tell me where she's going. Probably to Dad's, the one place she knows I won't follow.

I get directions to Amber's place. There isn't a lot to do here and I don't want to run the risk of Jasmine coming home and being difficult.

Amber's house is a gorgeous, ranch-style home on a big lot kind of in the middle of nowhere. It's a solid thirty minute drive from my place to hers with no traffic, so it has to take her at least that long to get to and from school every day. What a pain in the ass.

I wish I could become immune to the grand stature of houses in the nicer neighborhoods around Maple Burrow. Their towering rooftops, lean double-pane windows, metal-lined yards and the occasional stone fountain... I'm used to them, but I'm still a little envious.

Amber's house is different. Brick and wide, rather than painted and tall. Her driveway is cobblestone and forms a big circle around a brick planter with a fountain as the centerpiece. I don't entirely know where to park within that loop, so I pick a spot and hope it's kosher. God, I hope I wasn't expected to wear a dress. I feel like I should with how beautiful this house is. Or maybe cowboy boots, ha.

My hands are all sweaty. How attractive. I wipe them on my jeans before knocking, wondering if such a sound even reaches the furthest recesses of the house. A few moments later, Amber pulls open the door and I'm relieved to see she's in jeans and a t-shirt, just like me.

"You found it okay," she says, stepping back and into the house. "Come on in."

"Kind of hard to miss." I venture into the entryway, able to get a glimpse into a den or living room of some sort off to the left, and the largest flat-screen TV I've ever seen. Good Lord, my video games would look amazing on that. Come to mommy.

Amber shuffles down the entry hall and I follow like I'm afraid I might get lost if she gets too far ahead. She looks not unlike I see her every other day. She has this stick-straight brown hair, which kind of sounds unmemorable but is really quite pretty. Shiny. And really, really long. I can't believe I never realized it nearly reaches her waist.

Most of the house had hardwood flooring so I don't feel too guilty about not remembering to take my shoes off at the door, which is a habit Mom has engrained into me. Keeps the carpet from looking dirty or something.

"Your house is really pretty." How articulate am I? 'Really pretty'? I could have gone with 'fucking awesome' or 'fantastic' or even 'can your parents adopt me so I can live here?', but nooo.

"I like it," she admits, stepping into what is obviously her bedroom. "Beats living in the suburbs where your neighbors are breathing down your neck."

"I live in an apartment. Tell me about it." Her room is something spectacular. It's cool and woodsy, the walls a deep green, with white Christmas lights hang around the entire ceiling perimeter and window. The room itself is as big as my living room, but most of that is free floor space with a wide, circular, faux-fur brown carpet to occupy the center. Otherwise, her furniture is limited to a slightly messy desk complete with laptop, a bookshelf, and a bed.

I stare at the brown rug. "I feel like I ought to roll around in that to see if it's as soft as it looks."

Amber cracks a smile and sits down on it. "It is. Go ahead."

Don't need to be told twice. I plop down beside her and stretch out on my back, arms open snow angel style, and melt. I will be a puddle of goo. Very tricky to get out of fake fur. "Oh my god."

"Right?"

I sigh in contentment. "If anyone ever asks me what one item I would choose to take with me if I were stranded on a dessert island, this would be it."

"I'd bring my computer so I could order another one."

"But you wouldn't have internet access," I point out. Amber hmm's like she hadn't thought of that.

We sit in silence for awhile, which should be awkward but really isn't because it's a relaxed, sleepy sort of silence. I don't feel the need to talk about school or drama or much of anything, mainly because I'm still so talked out from last night.

When she does speak, it's to ask, "How was your double date?"

"It was a double date. I guess. How do they typically go?"

Her eyebrow lifts. "Like dates but with two couples instead of one, I would assume."

"Smartass." I draw my legs up to remove my boots so I can plant my feet in the carpet and wiggle my toes around. "I don't know. It was fun but bizarre. I wish we could have just called it a hanging out event rather than a double date."

"So you and Wade aren't actually dating?"

Natural reaction almost has me saying *what, no, of course not*, but then I remember. I'm not sure how to handle it when it's someone we interact with more. Brushing off the question isn't likely to work. "Uh... Maybe? I don't know." If I sounded any more convincing, I would cry.

"You're clearly thrilled about that."

"No, no, I am. He's a really nice guy."

"Yes, he is."

I peer up at her. "You don't have a thing for him, do you?" Just what I need. Upsetting my sister *and* someone I'm trying to be friends with.

Amber's face scrunches. "No. He's nice but I'm not interested. I didn't think you were, either."

I stare because I don't have an answer. I'm normally a good liar, so why is this so hard?

She continues, "It's none of my business," and, "sorry," before taking great interest in the state of her nails.

I roll onto my side, propping my head in my hand. "Who do you like, then?"

This, I feel, is a safer topic than it appears. Either Amber can tell me about whoever she does fancy, or...she's like me and never really been involved so it gives us something to bond over.

She rubs the side of her neck, head bowed, lashes lowered to half-mast. "No one."

"No one?"

"Anymore."

"But there was someone."

"Freshman year. He sort of killed my desire to get involved for awhile."

"Oh." Not as safe a subject as I thought. Clearly I am in desperate need of people skills. "Do you want to talk about it?"

"It's a pretty boring story," Amber says reluctantly.

"Says you. I like stories."

"Hm." When she draws her hand from her neck, her hair spills forward over her shoulder and mostly obscures her face from my view. "There was this guy...but he was dating someone else. I never really thought he'd pay me any attention, and I'd never go after someone taken." She speaks slow and careful, like her choice of words is of dire importance. "We talked a lot because we were lab partners, though. He asked to come over to work on a project one night and he told me him and his girlfriend had broken up and that he liked me."

"So...you got together?"

She takes a deep breath and straightens her spine, head tipping to cast her gaze to the ceiling. "No. Things...happened. Then the next day, I found out he'd never really broken up with his girlfriend at all and he pretended like I didn't exist."

I sit up to see her better, positioned so I have the perfect view of her profile. In that moment, she looks so sad and I can't for the life of me figure out who would use her like that. Even if we don't know each other that well, I know enough. I know she's quiet and shy, and she's not confident enough to get up on stage and perform. I know now she's the type of person who wouldn't screw around with someone if they were already involved, no matter how much she liked them.

And yet I don't know her well enough to know what to say. It was a few years ago, but I remember all too well the sting of rejection doesn't vanish overnight. Especially if this guy still goes to our school. It would break my heart to be in her position with Mara, and the sight of Mara's face would render the wound sharp and painful every time.

"I'm sorry," is all I can think to offer. "Not everyone is that big of a douche, though."

"I know that." She clears her throat like it will chase the pain from her voice. "I haven't met anyone since then I cared to bother with. Maybe in college."

"Won't be hard for you," I offer. "You're pretty, you're nice, and you're an artist. Guys dig artists." I think. Do they? Why wouldn't they?

Amber actually smiles. It's a dry, uncertain sort of smile but it's there. What is it with the people in my life? Between her and Wade, I feel I need to staple their mouths up into a permanent U so they don't look so beaten and sad all the time.

She says, "Thank you," but I don't know if she means it.

Amber's mom comes in to check on us. She's a plump lady with the same long, brown hair as Amber, and she's painfully nice. Marge is her name, and she owns and cooks at one of the nice restaurants in town. Can't say I've ever been there, but I smile when she tells me and pretend I'm impressed because it seems to be the polite thing to do.

Marge is the polar opposite of her daughter. She talks. A lot. She makes us some bizarre but tasty feta cheese dip with pita chips while she asks questions about me and what my parents do. These are the sorts of questions Amber would never ask, but I catch her looking mildly curious to see if I'll answer them anyway.

"Mom helps take care of an elderly lady part-time, but mostly she works at a diner downtown. Bruno's."

"Busy woman!" She has her back to us, washing dishes while we sit at the breakfast bar of their kitchen. "What about your dad?"

I swing my legs restlessly, nibbling on a pita chip. "We don't really talk much."

"Ohh." She says that one word, *ohh*, drawn-out like everything in the world makes sense. I try not to feel offended. "We see Amber's father so little with his job sometimes it's like he's not here at all."

If that was a lame attempt at connecting with me, I'm not sure I want it. There isn't an ounce of malice in her words, though, so I can't bring myself to be annoyed. She really is trying to be friendly. Those sorts of people are more frustrating than those who say things just to be jerks because you can't really snipe back at them.

Amber rolls her eyes and picks up the chips and bowl of dip. "We'll just take these outside. Thanks, Mom." She nods for me to grab our soda cans and leads me to the back porch. It's damp and cold, but not unbearable. We sit on a swinging bench with the food between us—which I'm still nomming on because it *is* delicious and I didn't eat breakfast—while staring out over the pool. It's a heated pool, she tells me, so it makes swimming in winter time bearable. Our apartment complex has a pool but it's closed more often than it's open. If not because of the cold weather, then because it's out of order. I think the office managers just don't like to upkeep it or worry about kids being loud.

After awhile Amber asks, "Why did you ask me to hang out?"

My mouth is full with chip and dip. It gives me a few second to think of an appropriate answer. "I don't know. I thought it would be fun. Do I need a reason?"

She purses her lips. "Do you consider this fun?"

That feels like a loaded question. I frown. "Yes, actually. It's relaxing." I fully mean that. Am I laughing until it aches like I was last night? No. But I'm really glad I forced myself not to cancel on her. Her house has a cozy, calm energy. I don't feel rushed or anxious here. Even if I'm still trying to work out Amber's moods and how to talk to her, I still find her company soothing, too.

"You're weird." She pops a chip into her mouth. "Good weird. I don't care much for going out. I don't like groups. Most people don't want to just...hang around someone's house all day and do nothing but talk and eat."

"Talking and eating are two of my favorite things," I admit. "Alongside video games and sleep. Maybe 'most people' need to learn to slow down a little and enjoy not constantly going and going."

"At our school, you get left behind if you're not constantly going and going."

"Then I'd rather get left." My shoulders rise and fall. "I want friends. I want people to talk to. But I don't want to do anything at someone else's pace."

She studies me, eyes half-lidded. It's a default look of hers; sleepy-eyed like she isn't interested in what you're saying, but she wouldn't be asking me if that were true. "Then why have you changed so much the last few years?"

The skin along the back of my neck prickles. "What do you mean? I haven't changed."

"Yes, you have." She draws her legs up, knees to her chest, fingertips tapping a rhythm on her thighs. "We had a class together freshman year. I don't think you remember. To be fair, I only remembered you because of your name. When you joined drama I got out my freshman yearbook and you looked so much different."

I was. My transition from Old-Me to High-School-Me started a few months into the year, long after yearbook photos were taken. I stare at a chip in my hand, watching a drop of dip fall to the patio.

"Then I remembered when I saw the picture. You had this wild hair and you always wore a lot of jewelry and neon shoes."

It's a period I don't enjoy being reminded of. The year I lost my sense of self. The year I slowly began to discard the things everyone always noticed about me. Stripped the color from my hair and let it grow out. Stopped wearing my fun clothes on casual Fridays. Bought a pair of black sneakers to replace my neon ones. By the end of the year, I looked like everyone else. The day I fully gave up trying to make new friends and be myself was the day I deleted Lisa and Delaine's numbers from my phone. I say nothing because any excuse I could give would be a lie. I don't feel Amber would buy into it, either.

"So which is it?" she presses. "Which London is the real one?"

This conversation shouldn't be happening. There is no answer I could give that would be correct. I only look at Amber with a smile that is only genuine because she cared enough to remember the old me.

"I thought I knew... But I'm not so sure anymore."

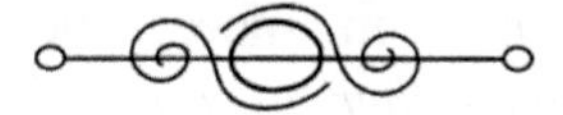

Mom is home that night and says Jazz went to Dad's for the weekend. She's gotten pretty good about not sounding despondent when she says that, but I know it bothers her and, like me, she'll never understand. Mom's always been big on encouraging my sister and me to make our own choices even if she doesn't always agree with them.

I make us dinner and we eat on the couch so Mom can catch up on some of her shows on the DVR. If it weren't for that thing, she'd never get a chance to see a full season of anything. Though I notice she's unusually quiet; Mom's not as talkative as Marge, but she likes to catch up with what I've been doing.

Especially since she knows I went out with friends two days in a row.

"What's wrong?" I ask around a forkful of spaghetti.

Mom wipes her mouth with a napkin. "Nothing. Just been a long couple of weeks, that's all."

She's my mom, so of course if something is really bothering her she's not likely to tell me. That's just how moms are. Well, it's how mine is, anyway. She'd rather shoulder everything alone rather than bother her daughters with it.

Still, as I take our empty bowls to the kitchen, Mom calls after me, "Have you noticed your sister acting any different lately?"

I pause, lingering by the end of the couch. "Lately being when? She's always pretty weird."

"Ever since she started taking her medication." Mom isn't looking at me. My first thought is, crap, she knows I took Jazz to get her meds refilled before she was due. That's hardly a criminal offense, right?

"I don't know," I admit. "Haven't noticed much difference."

Mom takes a deep breath. "Her doctor called. She's been making up excuses to get her prescriptions filled early."

Having my stomach flip-flop when full is not a pleasant feeling at all. "Excuses like what?"

"Saying she lost them. Saying she spilled water in her purse and they got ruined. They got stolen." There's a deep frown etched into her face like I haven't seen since....since Dad. Since she sat us down and said *girls, your father has a problem.*

I swallow the lump in my throat. There's something I've worried about, despite Jazz promising me it isn't true... "You think she's taking too many of them?"

"I don't know. I don't want to think that." She runs a hand back through her messy hair and sighs. "Don't worry about it, sweetheart. I'll talk to her, I just wanted to know if you had noticed anything."

"No." Should I admit to having helped Jazz that one time? I try to remind myself it doesn't matter because Mom already *knows*. Is it important how it happened once out of, apparently, several times? I'll chew on that guilt for awhile.

13

Monday morning I put serious thought into playing sick to get out of school. I'm eighteen, so I can technically call in myself without Mom's permission, but I can't find a way to justify it. I get up, get dressed, and get there without caving into my desire to run and hide.

Assuming the world is going to drastically change must've been pretty narcissistic of me. Nobody pays any more attention than they normally do. They look past me in the halls, bump into me while I'm trying to get into my locker. I'm starting to relax, thinking I was severely overreacting.

Until Wade steps up behind me and drops an arm around my shoulders. It's a simple gesture. To me and to him—*we* know it's a friendly sort of thing. No big deal. Yet I'm painfully aware that several people saw us and are now staring with open mouths and whispers on their tongues. We exchange slightly awkward greetings and he walks me to class. My face is red. I keep my chin up, avoiding gazes but refusing to be ashamed of carrying myself like I always have. This has to be just as uncomfortable for Wade as it is for me.

He takes me to homeroom and says he'll see me later. When I slide into my desk, the two girls who sit beside and in front of me twist around in their seats.

"Are you and Wade, like, dating?" one of them whispers.

I smile, forced, and lift a shoulder in a shrug.

They exchange curious looks. "I didn't even realize you knew him," the other says.

"We're in after school drama together." That's okay to admit, right? It's true, at any rate. "Is something wrong with that?"

Neither of these girls know what to make of me, I can tell. They look me over like they're trying to pick out one distinguishing feature that would make Wade want to date me. I know for a fact I'm nothing remarkable to look at. My hair is still a dull shade of platinum, but I never trimmed it as it grew out, so the layers lay kind of funny and my roots are horribly showing my natural dishwater blonde. I don't wear makeup aside from lip gloss. My shirt is wrinkled from sitting in the dryer all night. The uniform does nothing to accent my hips, which aren't so bad, but I'm kind of lacking in the boob department. Neither of them have any commentary to say to my face about all that, though; they straighten in their chairs as class begins.

It isn't the only time I get questioned throughout the day. I get asked in almost every class if I'm the girl dating Wade. Mara runs up to me in the halls, throwing her arms around my shoulders and squeezing, delighted by the news despite that I haven't actually confirmed it to anyone. At lunch, Wade sits with me in the courtyard I usually occupy. A place where it's always quiet and out of the way, where I think no one will bother us, and yet no less than three groups of curious onlookers wander by to say 'hi.' It's too much of a coincidence.

"You aren't eating," Wade comments.

"I think I've lost my appetite." I watch the most recent gaggle of girls pass, each casting their curious looks our way. "This doesn't bother you? Everyone *staring?"*

Wade steals my chips. I don't complain. Not like I'm going to eat them anyway. "I'm used to it."

"I don't know how you do it. It's been a day and already I'm sick of it."

He frowns. "Are you having second thoughts?"

I shake my head. "Made my choice. Can't very well back out of it now." Not yet, anyway. If things don't quiet down I might have to. We can say things weren't working and break up. This is high school where the average relationship lasts a month and a half

Wade looks down at his stolen chips like he, too, is losing his want to eat. "We could always not fake it."

I lay back on the bench we're eating on, staring at the sky. It's going to rain by the end of the day. "Huh?"

"As in, we could actually be boyfriend and girlfriend. If you wanted."

Only the sky sees the ridiculous expression that crosses my face. Except I don't get a chance to ask because the bell is ringing, and Wade is making quick work of gathering his things and muttering that he'll see me later.

Okay.

What just happened?

Does he realize what he said? He implied we should be real-dating instead of fake-dating. Clearly he's lost his mind. I'm seriously beginning to realize I don't have as good of a hold on Wade's train of thought as I thought I did.

Not much I can do about it, either. Not right now. All I can do is go to class and wait until after school to see him again. Even then it's not exactly a prime location for asking him anything because I'm running lines with Trevor today and Mara is busy gushing over how cute a couple she thinks Wade and I are. Oh, if only she knew.

The only person I get any sort of opportunity to talk to alone is, in fact, Trevor. Amber calls Mara and Wade off to help with the sets while Trevor struggles to remember his lines. He keeps apologizing, and I'm patient because at least it takes my mind off of other things.

After the fifth time in this scene where Trevor has to refer to his script, he sighs and plops down on the ground. "I'm so not built for this."

"It takes some getting used to," I offer. "What do you do when you're studying for a test and have to remember dates and stuff?"

He purses his lips. "I don't know. Usually Mara quizzes me, like with flash cards and stuff."

"You could do that with this, I guess. Write your lines on cards and have her quiz you with them."

"I think she's getting fed up trying to help me remember them." He gives me a sheepish grin. "She's still trying to remember all her own lines and she says it's distracting that I can't remember any of mine. Throws off her 'groove.'"

I can't imagine patient, sweet Mara saying something like that, but to be fair...what do I know? I have no clue what their relationship is like behind closed doors. However, I can't very well hear that and say 'oh, that's too bad.' "I could help, if you want?"

"Yeah?"

"I think I can clear time for you on my calendar."

"That'd be great." He considers. "Friday?"

Oh, me and my booming social schedule. Maybe I should at least pretend to think about if I have other things to do or not.

We make plans for Friday afternoon after school at his place. I've committed myself to an afternoon-slash-evening of rehearsing with Trevor and that makes me feel a little weird because I don't really know the guy, but I remind myself he's Mara's boyfriend and helping him out will help *her* out.

After drama, Wade walks me to my car. Faced with the chance of asking him what the hell he meant earlier, I almost don't want to. Things are getting really complicated really fast. But I do and Wade stops, leans back against my car, and sighs. "Just forget I said anything."

"No, I don't think I will. If we don't keep communication open on this thing, it's going to crash and burn."

"I just thought..." He runs a hand over his shaved head, flustered. "I haven't had a girlfriend since Freshman year. You haven't had a boyfriend. I meant it when I said I liked you, London. You're great." He looks at me as though hoping a compliment will placate me. I fold my arms. Not a chance. He continues, "Maybe we could give it a real chance and see if we can make things happen."

"Basically, you want to try fooling around with a girl to see if you can un-gay yourself, am I right?"

He sighs. "Yeah, I guess that's what I'm saying."

"*Really* doubt that's going to work. It's not some habit you can break, Wade."

"Isn't it worth a go?" He reaches for me, hands cupping my face. "I never tried it before because if I do and it doesn't work, whoever I was with would know. You're the only person I trust with this."

God damn him. He's so sincere and I don't doubt for a second that Wade would trade his left kidney for a chance to be what his family would consider *normal*. "This isn't a choice we made, feeling how we feel. Which is why I don't think trying to force it is going to do anything more than give us a headache."

His hands fall away from my face. "How do we know if we've never tried it?"

Okay, so he has a point there, more or less. I've never slept with a guy, never even kissed one. As a matter of fact, I've had more physical contact with Wade than I have with any other boy.

Yet I've never doubted my attraction to girls. There's just...something about them. Their curves and their smiles and their soft voices. Though it isn't like I can't find guys attractive, too. Like Wade. Wade is a cutie. But it's different. It isn't attraction, it's like...observation.

"I'm not dating you for real," is my final answer. His mouth downturns, and I continue, "But...we can try something. Just not here. For the record, I'm doing this for you and not for me, so don't expect some big epiphany on my part."

Wade doesn't look like he entirely understands, but he says okay and asks where. Which is a really good question. I'm not about to try anything at home where Jazz could potentially walk in and burst a blood vessel or something. Wade says he'll get back to me and we part ways, and I'm just glad the conversation is over. How in the world has my life gone from being a nobody to potentially making plans to try making out with a guy? Pretty sure this isn't how most girls go about it.

Coming home to the sound of a screaming match in the living room is so bizarre that I have to step back and check the number on our door to make sure I didn't walk into the wrong apartment. But there they are, Mom and Jazz, shouting at the top of their lungs. Well, Jazz is shouting. Mom is raising her voice, not quite yelling, but it's still really out of character. I think she's trying to be heard over Jazz's shrieks.

"I'm not lying! I'm *not lying*! Ask any one of my friends and they'll tell you—"

"—right, like your friends wouldn't lie to—"

"—don't know why I bother trying to tell you anything, Dad says—"

"Your dad is a manipulative asshole!"

Okay. *That* was a scream.

You could hear a pin drop onto plush carpet in the silence that follows. I ask, "What's for dinner?"

Both of them whirl around. Shame slides across Mom's face as she's instantly made aware of the noise they were making. Jazz stares right through me, seething, then spins on her heel and storms off. Mom calls, "We aren't done talking!"

"Yes," Jazz says. "We are. I'm going to stay with Dad!" She slams the bedroom door before we can react.

It's the quickest way to break Mom's spirit. Making her think that her daughters, who she's worked so hard to support, would ever choose their addict, loser father over her? I can see the weight of it crushing and draining the fight right out of her as she sinks onto the couch.

I sit on the coffee table so our kneecaps are touching, hands in my lap. I'm not so bad at comforting people, even if it makes me awkward. It's different when it's your mother. Were she a friend, I'd say *good riddance, let her go.* But this isn't a friend, and we're talking about my sister.

"I don't understand what's going on," she murmurs, wiping her eyes. "Why won't she talk to me?"

This isn't a question I have any answers for. "I can try talking to her."

Mom smiles fleetingly, patting my leg. "This isn't something for you to fix, London."

Except it should be. I feel like I'm the one to blame. Obviously something more is going on with Jazz than I ever expected and, unlike Mom, I see her on a regular basis. I should have noticed. I should have tried harder to talk to her instead of brushing it off because my poor, delicate little feelings were hurt.

Mom gets up and says she'll get something out for us to make for dinner. I take the opportunity to slip into the bedroom where Jazz is shoving clothes into a spare backpack. I open my mouth to speak and she cuts me off.

"Don't fucking talk to me."

My eyebrows shoot up. "Wow, okay. Rude. What's your problem? She's worried about you."

She glares. "It's really no one's business, is it?"

"Uh...she *is* our mother so it kind of is. You realize you broke her heart with that whole Dad comment, right?"

"I meant it." She's running out of room in her backpack. Her face scrunches up. Not sure she realized how much she'd be forced to leave behind if she stormed out like she's doing. "At least at Dad's, I have money to go out with my friends and he doesn't constantly breathe down my fucking neck."

"No, he just forgets to pay his utilities and his rent and buy groceries."

She lurches to her feet. "You have *no idea* what he does now. You never talk to him!"

I level an unimpressed look in her direction, leaning back against the door. "Tell me I'm wrong."

It's that simple. Jazz has had plenty of opportunity to tell me that Dad is doing better, being a responsible adult, but she never has. This leads me to think he's still barely scraping by, just like he always has. Moving from job to job. Borrowing money he doesn’t intend to pay back. Even now Jazz doesn't defend him. She could try lying, but she's a horrible liar and I would know. She turns her back on me to cram a few pairs of socks into her backpack, which she then struggles to zip up.

"Look, why don't you take a little bit to calm down and then try talking to Mom again?" I run a hand through my hair with a sigh. "I know you're pissed off, but you two should really have a civil conversation. If you think she's not getting it, then explain it to her."

Jazz flings the bag over her shoulder and gives a flick of her hand, a dismissive gesture telling me to get out of her way.

I don't.

Now she's just pissing me off.

"*Move,*" Jazz growls.

"You're being a really big brat right now, do you know that?"

"Go to hell."

God, I want to grab her head and shake her until something rattles into place. "Are you stupid? We're trying to take *your side* and you're not exactly giving us a reason to."

"Nothing is going on. Just leave me alone!"

Everything happens at once. Jazz grabs my arm and tries to tear me away from the door so she can get out. I shove her without thinking. Automatic response. Reflex. She throws a punch, knuckles clipping my shoulder.

Then it's *on.*

We're on the floor, kicking and hitting and pulling. She's trying to ruin my face. I'm trying to pin her down. We might be evenly matched given our similar height and weight, but we'll never find out. Mom flings the door open behind us and before I know it, she's managed to pry us apart so we're both on our asses on the ground with her as the barrier between us.

"What is wrong with you two?!"

Jazz's hair is a frazzled mess. She glares past Mom at me like she wants an excuse to pick up where we left off. Instead she gets up, grabs her bags, and stomps out of the room. For some reason I don't begin to comprehend, Mom lets her go without a word.

My scalp is throbbing where Jasmine damn near yanked my hair out. Otherwise the only thing injured is my pride. And my feelings. My eyes start to water, mouth twisting in the tell-tale sign I'm about to start sobbing. Mom kneels and puts her arms around me. I think she might be crying, too, because neither of us have a clue what to do now.

We spend a quiet evening in front of the TV with the frozen pizza I made. Mom doesn't eat much. She's probably worried about Jazz out there alone, trying to get to Dad's. I'm sure even deadbeat Dad wouldn't have left his daughter to walk alone in the dark, but not sure enough to bet on it. Before bed, I'll swallow my pride and text Jazz to make sure she got there in one piece.

Mom calls it a night early. I haven't even touched my homework, ugh. I bring a slice of pizza back to the dining table and unload my books and papers. It's hard to focus on numbers and words when so much is going on to disrupt my usual state of calm.

You know, I have friends. Friends I could potentially call and talk to about my problems and feel better. Then it occurs to me I don't feel close enough with any of them except maybe Wade, but I'm kind of avoiding him because of this whole boyfriend/girlfriend thing. I force myself to finish up my homework—one less thing to bite me in the ass later—and as a reward I text Mara to say hi and see what she's up to. Usually she texts me first, and it's only been a very small number of times. Three, maybe four. The conversation never seems to last long, and I've been too nervous about coming across as a creeper by initiating anything.

Thankfully, she writes back quickly and doesn't seem annoyed.

Just had yummy dinner. U??

Maybe it's better I don't talk to anyone on the phone. It's easier to lie through words on a screen and keep up a face that nothing is wrong. *Homework. Ugh. Want to hang out?*

It's a little while before she writes back: *me & Trevor were going to a movie do u want to come?*

I respond: *No, that's ok. See you guys tomorrow.*

So much for that. It's sweet of her to invite me along, though who knows if it's only Mara being polite rather than being interested in hanging out with me. I'm not up for being around Trevor. Maybe I'm not even up for being around Mara. I want company and I want to be alone. I want to be social and I want solitude.

This having friends thing is complicated.

14

Jazz isn't at school the next day. I scour all her usual before-school loitering spots with no sign of her. Since some of her friends are staring in my direction when I pass by, I even ask them if they've seen her. No go. She texted me last night with a curt message that she got to Dad's fine so I know she's okay. Mom isn't going to be happy she skipped school. She'll be less happy that Dad allowed it.

If this keeps up, things are going to get ugly. Mom and Dad technically have joint custody of us because Mom was trying to be kind and, at the time, Dad was making an effort to get better and put himself through rehab. She could change that, but I know she doesn't want to and, more than that, I know she can't afford to.

I hate Dad. Right now, I kind of hate Jazz. I'll hate her more if she pushes Mom to make a decision like that.

The only person I really feel I can talk to about this is Wade, even if I'm dreading picking up our dating conversation. When I find him he's rummaging around in his locker and there's a girl whose face I only vaguely recognize—Melody? Mary? I don't remember—talking to him. Or at him, rather. Wade looks like he wishes she'd go away, or that he could leave without coming across as rude.

Our eyes meet rather coincidentally and his face lights up. He's so relieved to see me that I can't bring myself to abandon him there, so I approach with a smile firmly in place.

"Hey, good morning. Am I interrupting?"

Wade puts an arm around my shoulder. "No, not at all. London, this is Missy, Allen's girlfriend. Missy, you know London, don't you?"

Missy. I knew it started with an M. Allen, if I’m remembering correctly, is one of the guys on Wade and Trevor’s swim team.

Missy's smile is friendly enough but there's something about it that doesn't come across terribly sincere. "I think everyone in school knows her now."

I refuse to let myself look terrified by this comment. "Should I be worried?"

"Not at all." Her face is that of a porcelain doll: small lips and big eyes, tiny smile painted in place and never wavering. She’s beautiful in a fashion model magazine kind of way. "Why wouldn't we know Wade's girlfriend, of all people? You just seemed to fall out of the sky."

How do I respond in a way that wouldn't be catty or bitchy? "Yeah, it was a long drop." I turn to Wade. "Walk me to class?"

Wade doesn't seem to know what to say. He just nods, hugs me against his side, and leads me away.

I can't help but admit, "I'm getting real tired of everyone's attitudes."

"It's something new for all of them," Wade assures. "They'll get over it. And...thanks for saving me back there."

"Don't mention it." We turn the corner, out of Missy's line of sight. I consider shrugging Wade's arm off, but I decide against it. I kind of want to hug him just because a hug sounds nice right about now.

"You all right?" he asks.

"Why wouldn't I be?"

"You're all tense." He squeezes my shoulder, thumb pressing into an achy muscle and making me wince. "Did something happen?"

We stop in the hall outside my class and I almost tell him all about the previous night. Except it would mean confessing about *why* Jazz was mad, and how Mom and I think she's abusing her meds. “Family issues,” is all I say with a weak smile and a shrug, and Wade gives me a sympathetic look that says he knows I’m downplaying it and there’s a story I’m not telling, but he doesn’t push.

I wish I could be attracted to Wade. Not because it would be 'easy' or 'normal,' but because he's him. He makes me feel like I matter. Like my problems aren't something insignificant and stupid but that he respects my privacy. I can only hope I make him feel the same. Maybe that's why he wants to try *actually* dating. Because he wants this thing between us to be more than what it is.

I don't think he realizes what we're feeling is what friends—good friends—*should* feel toward one another. Which is sad because it means neither of us have a good friend other than each other. Doubly sad because we've barely been friends for a few weeks now.

Wade asks, "Is there anything I can do?" and I shake my head and then lay it on his shoulder, disappointed he doesn't have some miraculous answer for me, but what was I expecting? At least I feel better having talked about it.

The final bell rings and I pull away. Before I can disappear into class, Wade asks, "Tonight?" It takes me a second to realize what he means. Tonight. I promised, didn't I? Which makes my insides start up with the acrobatics, but I smile none the less.

"Text me the details."

'The details' are nothing more than: *my place, after school.* Which means two things. (1) I'm probably not going to have a chance to freshen up at home before we do...whatever it is we're going to do and (2) I'm actually going to get to see Wade's house. Weird.

Number one makes me ridiculously self-conscious. It would be nice to at least...I don't know. Brush my teeth or something. Now I'm afraid to even eat lunch. I also feel I should be wearing something nicer than a stupid school uniform, or at least a matching bra and panties. Not that he's going to be seeing them, but you know. It would give me some internal sexy points and I could stand to have some of those right now.

Wade and Trevor are off at swim practice again. Mara cuts out early to go watch them while Amber works on props and I recite lines at her while sewing buttons on a costume. She doesn't once complain about my talking, and even corrects me here and there, telling me where my words are stiff and unconvincing.

After repeating the same monologue over and over for fifteen minutes straight, I groan and flop backward onto the stage floor. My neck has a crick in it from hunching over and I still have two other dresses that need buttons. Amber leans over me, nudging her glasses up.

"Dying?"

"My throat is." I try to stretch out my spine, shoulders pressing back into the worn wood. "Pain in the ass, man. What made me think doing costumes *and* learning lines was a great idea?"

"Because you want people to like you," Amber replies easily. That gets my attention. I stare at her. She stares back. "Isn't that what it is? You were like this eager, excited puppy coming in here that day."

My nose wrinkles. "Rude. I'm more like a cat. All elegance and grace."

Amber snorts.

"Double-rude." I fold my hands behind my head and grin. "When are we gonna hang out again? You can come to my place this time, if you want. I don't have a flat-screen or a mom who cooks but, you know."

Her eyes are downcast, focusing back on her painting. "You want to hang out with me again?"

"That's...sort of why I asked. Why? Is that bad?"

She shakes her head. It's a shame she keeps her hair tied up so often because it's gorgeous, but at least this way she isn't using it to hide her face. "That'd be cool."

"We could grab some movies. I can cook. Have a nice night in?"

"Sounds like a date."

I look at her. Really look at her. I guess it is kind of date like. That is, if a guy and a girl made these plans it would most certainly be considered a date but because we're girls, it's not. Right? Right. I wonder how I'm ever going to manage a real date if

I don't even begin to know how to ask a girl out properly. "Saturday?"

Amber agrees, "Saturday."

She takes a break from her painting to help me sew buttons. It's nice to not have to talk about anything at all. Afterward, I hang around outside until Wade is done with swim practice. He greets me with a forced and uncomfortable smile. He offers to drive and bring me back later for my car, but I assure him I'd rather drive myself, even at the expense of gas money. I don't like being somewhere without my car in the event I want to leave. When you get used to having that kind of freedom, it's uncomfortable to have it revoked.

Besides, I need the fifteen minute drive to gather my thoughts and determine if I'm really going to do this. It's not like I told him I'd have sex with him, but I did insinuate we could just...what, 'try something'? What does that entail? Cuddling on the couch and hair-petting? Making out? Really should have clarified all this so I don't feel so utterly nauseous and worried I'm going to mess something up by the time we arrive at his place.

Wade's house is everything I thought it would be. Huge. Gorgeous. With a sprawling front yard and meticulous landscaping. The windows are all dark, leading me to think no one is home. That's why he invited me over, right? So we would be alone?

Wade takes off his shoes just inside the front door and I do the same. My socks don't match. Why couldn't I have taken ten extra seconds to fix that this morning? The entryway opens into a spacious living room that doesn't look like it gets much use. I find out in a moment it doesn't, because it's a sitting room. A secondary living room. For sitting. With guests. What?

The real living room—complete with television and at least slightly more used furniture—is further into the house. This is where Wade takes me and gestures around somewhat awkwardly.

"Uh...here's my place. Do you want a tour?"

"We don't have all night," I tease. But I am drawn to the fireplace where the mantel is neatly lined with frames. "This is your family?"

Wade steps up beside me. "Yeah. That's my Mom and my Dad." He points to one that looks like a family Christmas photo wherein he's standing with two other boys that can only be his brothers. "That's David and Antoine."

"Do they live here?"

"David has a place out in New York and comes back for holidays. Antoine's in grad school, so he's here some weekends and vacations." He shrugs.

"I always thought being the baby of the family would be nice."

"Maybe for you."

"Yeah, for me." I pick up the photo, examining it closer, and then return it to its place on the mantel. Everything in here is so clean that there isn't even a line of dust where the frames are sitting. "Jazz got away with everything growing up. I mean, Mom's pretty laid back, but still."

"Not like that here," Wade says solemnly. "I've got two brothers who are successful and my parents' idea of perfection. I have to live up to that."

I've gathered as much about his family life but it's different hearing Wade actually say it. I look up at him. "Which means finding some nice girl they approve of and settling down and all that."

His gaze doesn't leave the photos. "Pretty much, yeah."

I look at his parents in the pictures. They both stand straight, shoulders back, clothes neat and tidy, and their smiles look almost practiced. They don't look like the kind of people who would react well to finding out their son is gay, and it's hard for me to imagine a parent turning their back on their kid like I think Wade's parents might do.

Wade takes a deep breath. He reaches for my hand. His thumb slides across my knuckles and it's nice, pleasant, but it's not like my heart starts dancing or anything. Because this is Wade. My friend. And that's all we're ever going to be. I'm aware he's leaning in to kiss me and that I told him I would so taking it back now seems cruel after I've come all this way, and I guess some small part of me is curious to see if this will work. Don't knock it 'til you try it, right?

So I let his lips brush against mine. Briefly and lightly at first, then again with more courage once he realizes I'm not going to hit him. I've never kissed anyone before, which means my brain is thinking too much about all these little sensations and how I'm moving, how I'm kissing him back to make sure I'm...I don't know, doing it right? I bet the book store has manuals on how to kiss. I bet I should not be thinking so much about kissing while kissing.

Wade slips his arms around my waist. I put my hands on his shoulders because I'm not sure what else to do with them. His mouth is really soft and really warm, a nice combination that makes me wonder if kissing a girl would be like this, too. All soft and delicate. Also makes me wonder if Wade is thinking the same thing: if kissing me is like kissing a guy. If there's a guy in particular he has in mind.

The thought has me smiling despite myself. Smiling, and then giggling, which is not an okay thing to be doing while kissing, I think. Fortunately for me, Wade also starts to smile. We pull apart, laughing as we realize how utterly idiotic this entire idea was.

"That was..."

"Weird?" Wade finishes.

"Not *bad* weird," I say, not wanting to hurt his feelings. "Just...you know."

"No, I get it." He's still smiling, amused but a touch sad. I'll bet he wanted this to go better than it did. "It was worth a try. I'm sorry I made you do it."

"You didn't make me do it." I shrug. "Who knows? We could've felt sparks and realized we're madly in love with each other or something. I'm sure stranger stuff has happened."

He shakes his head, embarrassed. "Still sorry."

I put some distance between us and have a seat on the couch. "The person you should be kissing is a nice guy. Bonus points for hotness."

Running a hand over his face, Wade sits beside me, still granting that polite bit of space between our persons. "Right. I'll go grab the first cute guy I see and ask him if he wants to make out with me."

I grin at the thought. "Not quite what I had in mind, but it could work."

"Too risky, London. I can't." He tips his head back, studying the ceiling. "I can't let something like that happen."

"Because of your family? Then don't tell them. They don't need to know right now."

"They would find out. Because the person I'm interested in sure as hell isn't...isn't like me. Besides, high school is almost over. I'll be going away for college so what's the point of ruining my life for a relationship I'll have to end in a few months anyway?"

My nose wrinkles. "You are the most cynical person...wait, wait. You said 'the person I'm interested in.' Does that mean there's—"

He silences me with a sharp look. "I didn't mean—no. We're not discussing it."

I bite my lip, wracking my brain for any names or faces I've seen Wade talk to at school. Maybe on the swim team? Or it could be someone who doesn't even go to our school. Wade has plenty of outside activities and he's a regular at church every Sunday. If he doesn't want to talk about it, I'm not going to force him. Instead I scoot closer and throw my arms around his neck, planting a friendly kiss on his cheek.

"You'll find someone you can walk up to and kiss whenever you want. Don't give up on that. Please?"

Because if there's no hope for Wade, what hope is there for me?

15

Jasmine still isn't at school the following day. Her phone is ringing, which means it's on, but she keeps sending my calls to voicemail. I know Mom has plans on calling Dad if Jazz isn't home by the weekend, but I don't want it to come to that. Which means taking it upon myself, I guess.

I've only been to Dad's apartment once when Jazz begged me to drop her off on a rainy night. It's been nearly a year and I'm flying by memory alone. I will say this: Dad's apartment complex makes mine look like the Hilton. I knock on the wrong door at first, but when I tell the lady that answers who I'm looking for she pulls a face and points to the apartment above her own. No idea what kind of car Dad drives these days, so I don't know if he's home. I'm keeping my fingers crossed as I knock on the right door that he's not.

Jazz answers with her hair pulled back, looking a bit bedraggled and—at first I think it's the lighting, but it's not—a bit of a bruise on her cheek. Her face blanches at the sight of me and I think if I didn't move so quickly to step inside, she might have shut the door in my face.

"What are you doing here?" she asks at the same time I ask, "What happened to your face?"

She turns away and slinks back to the kitchen, where she has chicken frying in a pan. God, this place is yuck. The carpets are stained. The paint is faded and chipping. It's free of clutter. If Dad has anything going for him, it's the fact that he's a pretty clean guy. Not really one to leave stuff lying around. But even though it looks like the floor has been recently vacuumed and it doesn't smell dusty, it just...*feels* dirty. I can imagine walking out here in the middle of the night and flicking on a light only to witness a hoard of cockroaches scattering.

"Seriously, Jazz, what happened to your face?" I reach out to touch my fingers to her jaw and she flinches away. "Did Dad hit you?"

"He slapped me," she corrects, patient and nonchalant like it's no big deal. "You would've been pissed, too, if someone showed up at your house in the middle of the night and woke you up out of a dead sleep."

This must be why she hasn't come to school. The bruising isn't terribly pronounced, but it's enough to make people ask questions. She forgot her makeup bag at our place. No way to cover it. My stomach turns. My heart is in my throat. Why does she let him get away with these things? Why does she justify it and take the blame as something she did?

I turn away from my sister and check out the rest of the apartment even as Jazz asks, "What're you doing?" in that worried tone that suggests she knows I'll find something I don't want to find.

"Giving myself a tour." By the looks of it, Jazz sleeps on the couch and Dad gets the bedroom. I head for the bathroom, investigating the medicine cabinet and beneath the sink. There really isn't much. Some of Jazz's medicine and typical stuff you'd find in anyone's cabinets. Cold meds, some band aids, antacid.

Then I look into the trash can next to the toilet. Jackpot. Inside are a collection of prescription meds. Some are Jasmine's. Some are made out to people I don't know. I snatch up the bin as Jazz appears in the doorway behind me, mouth downturned.

"He's clean, huh?" I ask dryly.

Jazz's eyes are downcast. "They're anti-depressants and stuff for his anxiety," she mumbles. "The doctors won't prescribe him any of his own."

"Probably because he's a fucking pill addict and he's abusing them."

"He needs them to *function,* London!"

"What a load of bull shit." My voice is shaking. Mom and I were wrong. We were so, so wrong. Jasmine isn't the one abusing her medicine. Dad is. I can hardly see anything except the image of my dad downing my sister's pills while she's left to suffer without it. No wonder she's been a basket case. The only thing worse than taking her off of them completely is her going on and off of them repeatedly. "What's he paying you per bottle, huh? What's he doing now that the doctors have cut you off?"

She only stares at me for half a second before turning away. I follow her to the kitchen where her chicken is burning. She moves the pan to safety. I overturn the trashcan on the counter. Bottles hit the linoleum and roll every direction.

"Come on. Look at this and tell me he's not abusing this stuff!"

Jazz whirls on me. "It's better than what he's like when he's not on anything, okay? Because then he just...lies around and he won't get out of bed. He wasn't working, he wasn't paying his bills. He was wasting away." She slams the cooking tongs in her hand to the countertop. "All he needs is for someone to be there for him! He didn't have Mom, he didn't have you. Who else was supposed to take care of him?"

The tears on Jasmine's face aren't angry tears like I'm used to. They're tired tears from someone who's been trying to do what she thinks is right but hasn't had anyone to talk to about it. Certainly she hasn't been talking to her friends about Dad. Not to me. Not to Mom.

I pull Jazz into my arms. She resists at first. Then when she realizes I'm not letting go, she buries her heavy sobs into my shoulder. I can blame her for making stupid decisions and not talking to us about what's happening, but I can't blame her for her unwavering loyalty to someone she cares about. I'm not so sure I could ever turn a blind eye to her or Mom suffering, and God knows I've witnessed them in enough pain over the years. Some of it a result of their own stubbornness and bad choices.

But—"It shouldn't be you," I murmur against her hair. "It isn't your job to take care of him. He has to take care of himself. It isn't fair to you, Jazz."

She pulls back, red eyed and blotchy faced, shaking her head. "You don't get it."

I rub her arms and use my jacket sleeve to wipe at her tears. "I *do* get it. Trust me, I do. He'll never get better as long as he has people enabling him."

There's a nod that I'm hoping means she *really* hears me and understands. Maybe she'll come home with me. Maybe we can talk to Mom and, together, there's something we can do to help without dragging all of us under like Dad is so good at doing. Instead, she says, "You should go. He'll be home any minute and I need to get dinner finished."

"Come home with me," I plead.

"Not today. For the weekend, maybe." She wipes at her eyes, sniffs, and turns away from me. "I'll be at school tomorrow so tell Mom not to freak out."

I debate if I could possibly wrestle Jazz into the car and drag her home. Yet what good would it do? She would leave again the moment my back was turned and then I'd really never get her to come home.

I'm at a loss. No choice, huh? Except to leave. My steps are slow and mechanical as I make my way down the stairs to the parking lot, throwing repeated looks over my shoulder like I expect Jazz to change her mind and she'll come running out of the apartment any minute. She doesn't.

As I'm about to unlock the car I hear, "London?" and my spine goes rigid.

I haven't seen my father face to face in over a year. Even then it was a brief moment wherein I swore I'd never lay eyes on him again. I'm completely loathed to turn around and see him standing there, keys in hand. Looking surprisingly normal. Grayer than I remember, but otherwise the same. Which only pisses me off further. He's graduated from hard drugs that make him look like shit and moved on to pills that haven't yet had too much of an effect on his appearance. From the glazed look in his eyes, I also know he's on something right now. Good old Dad.

"Your hair is growing out," he says with a smile.

I don't try to return it. Without taking my eyes off him, I jam the keys into the car door, intending on getting in and driving off without a word.

Dad scoffs. "Oh, come on, Lon. I haven't seen you in...how many months? Why don't you come in for a bit?"

I wanted to be quiet for Jazz's sake and to avoid any drama she might get caught up in. But when he reaches for my arm I turn around and smack his hand so hard it slams into the side view mirror. He jerks back, shocked and more than a little pissed off. I refuse to stand down.

"Don't. Touch. Me."

Dad takes a deep breath and points a finger in my face. "You better check that attitude, little lady. Just because we haven't spoken doesn't mean a thing. I'm still your father."

"Screw you," I snarl. "Who do you think you are, laying a hand on her? Huh? Doing it to Mom wasn't enough? Now you hit your own daughter because she doesn't have the drugs to keep you wasted?"

He takes a step back like he expects me to lash out. I've never wanted to hurt someone so badly. What I wouldn't give to throw him down and grind his face into the sidewalk. See how he likes it. But doing so would prove that I am my father's daughter, solving things with violence, and I refuse. I absolutely refuse.

"London," he warns.

I yank open the car door and point at him. I'm not above threats. "I swear to God, if you touch her again I will *ruin your life*. I will make you regret waking up every day."

Dad doesn't say anything as I get behind the wheel and peel out of the parking lot.

Halfway down the street I burst into tears. Shaking. Can't breathe. I pull to the side of the road and let it out, sobbing hysterically with my forehead against the wheel. Remembering a hundred things I'd rather not remember.

Not all of them are bad.

That's what makes it so fucking hard.

I remember Dad picking me up from school. Hugging and kissing me and listening with all smiles as I babbled about my day. Sometimes he'd take me for ice cream. "*Don't tell Mom I spoiled your dinner.*" He never missed a school play like Mom did. He never missed anything. He was always there while Mom was busy with work.

In hindsight, I recognize this was only because he couldn't keep a job and was steadily spiraling down into his addiction. Mom had to work and miss things *because* of Dad. She never said as much, never used it as an excuse or justification. She always smiled sadly and apologized. I used to tell her how mad I was at her for missing all the important moments of my life. I've made my mother feel guilty for the faults of my father. I am a terrible daughter.

How is it possible to hate someone so much? Especially when that person is half of who you are?

Again I desperately want to call someone just to talk. I consider Mara, but in scrolling through my contacts I see Amber's name and I linger on it. Mara really knows nothing about me, and Wade has so much of his own stuff to deal with... Amber might listen.

I wait until I can at least breathe without sniffling before dialing. Amber answers on the second ring. "Hey." Casual, like we do this every day.

The sound of her voices chokes me up all over again. "Hey. What's up?"

"Not much." She pauses, chewing something. "You all right?"

New tears spill from my eyes to replace the old ones. My voice catches on a hiccup of emotion. "Um... Bad day."

This time, Amber sounds sincerely worried. "What happened?"

Telling her would be an invasion of Jazz and Mom's privacy, wouldn't it? Airing our dirty laundry or whatever. "Just...my dad. Stupid stuff." I'm a moron. What was I hoping to achieve with this conversation? "I'm sorry. I should let you go."

"Don't be a pain. Talk to me. Do you want some company?"

I bite at my lip until it hurts. Truthfully... "I think I'd like that."

Amber keeps me on the phone until I've calmed down enough to drive, then I give her my address and head home. She lives far enough away that I have a chance to get myself cleaned up, splashing cold water on my face so I'm not such a wreck, and straighten the apartment. Mom will be home later but by then I hope to be not so obviously recovering from an emotional nuclear meltdown.

When Amber arrives, I let her in with a forced smile. Her hair is down again and I think I should tell her sometime she has such pretty hair and that I wish she'd leave it down more often. "I've got sandwich stuff for dinner, if you're hungry," I offer, leading her into the kitchen. "Sorry, but I'm not as good a cook as your mom."

She snorts, peeling out of her jacket and looking around. I'm too tired to care what she thinks about my place compared to hers. Or maybe I'm confident enough that Amber isn't the sort of person to judge. "Sandwiches are fine."

We hang out in the kitchen, putting together sandwiches and chips and sodas, not even bothering to sit down while we eat. I'm not honestly very hungry; it's just something to do with my hands and to occupy my brain for a bit.

Amber licks a spot of mustard from the side of her thumb and dusts off her crumby hands over the sink. "So, do you want to talk about it?"

I stare down at my own half-eaten food. "I don't know."

"Might make you feel better."

"Might make me feel like I'm whining."

She shrugs. "It isn't whining if someone asks you about it, I think. You said it was your dad. He doesn't live here, does he?"

I glance over. "How do you know that?"

"Pictures in the dining room are all of you, Jasmine, and your mom. Plus I don't think you've ever really mentioned your dad before tonight. I sort of assumed he was completely out of the picture."

Oh. That would do it, huh? I give up trying to eat and set the plate aside, resting back against the counter. Amber leans right next to me. We're hip to hip, both staring at our feet, and I don't know why but I'm compelled to simply...rest my head on her shoulder. After a moment, her head drops to lie atop mine. The position might be a little awkward but it's comfortable, and after a few moments I'm able to open my mouth and start telling her about Dad.

No, not just Dad. But Jazz and Mom and everything that happened tonight. I tell her how I'm scared Jazz is going to want to stay with Dad to take care of him no matter how much it hurts her. I tell her how I'm scared for Mom because she's always so damned tired and I don't ever want to let her down or disappoint her. I tell her about the fights, the arguments over the last several weeks. Amber listens to it all in complete silence, but I can tell she's paying attention. Her arm slides around my shoulders, hugging me to her side, and I never realized how badly I wanted a hug until now.

When I'm finished, all she has to say is, "You've had a lot going on."

She doesn't know the half of it. It's not like I can tell her about Wade or about my crush on Mara. "Jazz is the one who's had a lot going on."

"Don't act like your problems don't matter, London." The arm around my shoulders tightens briefly. "Don't sell yourself short. You're trying to play mom to your little sister to protect your mother, and I think that's admirable."

I sniff a bit. Thankfully, I'm pretty cried out from earlier in the car. I don't really feel like breaking into messy sobs in front of anyone, even Amber. "I have no idea what I'm supposed to do."

"Honestly? I don't know." She pulls away, turning to face me. "Sorry. I'm kind of shit at giving advice."

"Maybe advice wasn't what I needed so much as just...talking about it." I shake my head. "So thanks."

Amber lifts one shoulder in a shrug. "Not that I mind lending an ear, but isn't this the sort of thing boyfriends should be for?"

"I don't have a..." The words spill out of my mouth faster than I can remember that, yes, I technically *do* have a boyfriend. I'm stuck staring at Amber while she squints at me, and we're both confused but for entirely different reasons. Her because of my slip-up. Me because...I'm really, really tempted to tell her the truth.

Instead I smile as best as I can. "Guess I'm still not used to that. I don't know. Wade's got a lot going on, you know?"

"I wouldn't have a clue what Wade has going on." She turns away, reaching for her soda.

I wonder what Amber would say if I told her Wade and I are faking it. If I could come up with a plausible excuse, I think I just might. Shy of telling her the total truth, though, I can't think of a single logical reason why a guy and a girl would pretend to date and lie to even their friends about it.

Therefore, Wade is a topic I would rather avoid. Amber doesn't bring it up again. We take the remainder of our food to the living room, park on the couch, and spend our evening with crime shows and badly narrated documentaries. I'm starting to feel better, and Amber's laugh is my cure.

16

Diary of a Noble

Normally I use this blog as a sort of outlet for saying things I can't say to anyone in person. Things I can't tell my Mom or J. I can throw this stuff out into the internet because it's kinda like screaming into the void. I get a few comments here and there and—no offense, you're all lovely—but seeing words typed on a screen isn't the same thing as someone being able to reach out and hold you, a voice against your ear letting you know everything will be okay. Having that with A was really...nice. I haven't had a real friend do something like that for me since middle school.

But then I feel kind of guilty. Are we really *real* friends if I'm not entirely honest with her about things? If I were to find out she was lying about something so important, my feelings would be really hurt.

Funny that my concern has shifted. I'm no longer as worried about Mara finding out as I am Amber. I wonder why that is?

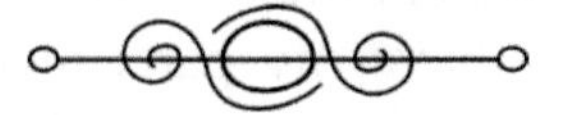

The rest of the week presents me with little to no time for dwelling on my situation. Wade and Trevor are busy with practice so it's mainly Mara, Amber and me working on sets and running lines after school. I'm busy enough that when Friday rolls around, I've totally spaced the fact that I'm supposed to go to Trevor's tonight. I'm halfway home when he texts a reminder, and then I'm cursing and pulling into the nearest driveway to turn around and head to his place. I never even got the chance to tell anyone I'd be here. The thought never really crossed my mind that it might matter.

Trevor's house isn't as big as Wade's or Amber's, but it's still a hell of a lot larger than mine and everything inside of it is neat and well-kept. I've seen the state of Trevor's locker before, so I'm willing to bet either his parents are the neat freaks, or they have a housekeeping service. He lets me in and leads me upstairs to his room, depositing his bag onto the floor. "Can I get you anything to eat or drink?"

I set my own bag next to his, looking around. Typical boy's room. Or at least, what I would expect Trevor's room to look like. Standard, non-descript blue bedding, kick-boxing and NFL magazines atop the dresser, a pile of shoes at the foot of his bed. He has more shoes than Jazz and I put together, geez. "Uh, no thanks. I'm good." Too nervous, rather. I don't feel the same level of comfort here that I do at Amber or Wade's houses. "Your family isn't home?"

"Nah, it'll be a few hours." He takes a seat on the edge of his bed. I look at him and think...maybe that's what bothers me. That we're here in his room instead of downstairs in the cozy-looking living room. It just doesn't feel right, I guess, being alone with a guy I'm not really familiar with. In his bedroom. When no one else is home.

"Okay. Then should we get started?" The sooner we practice, the sooner I can leave.

"Oh, yeah, yeah." Trevor claps his hands on his knees and retrieves a copy of the script from his bag. "The third act is where I'm having problems."

Weird considering I'm the one with all the lines in that act, but whatever. I already have my parts memorized so I take the script out of his hands and flip to the part in question. It's the act where Mable and Joseph have their big confrontation after Mable's kiss with Anna. Trevor is watching me, so I guess I ought to pick a line and start.

We spend the next thirty minutes practicing, with Trevor stumbling over his lines again and again while I gently correct him. Close to the hour mark, I think we're finally making significant progress and we're actually having fun. It helps that I really like how Wade has written Mable. Like he wrote her just for me. She's eccentric and proud, confident, and when I get really into it it's a huge relief to slip into someone else's skin for a while. I'm not looking at Trevor anymore. I'm looking at *Joseph.* A man I have feelings for and yet my job comes first.

"I will not!" I say hotly, spanning the space of the room with the script all but forgotten. I don't need it. Trevor almost doesn't anymore, either. "You would leave a woman who loves you for me, but what of my feelings? You have nothing to offer me, dear Joseph. Nothing that I cannot attain with my own...assets."

Trevor circles me and he's adjusted to his role, isn't so stiff and awkward in his movements anymore. "I have plenty to offer you," he says, and leans in close. I don't think about it. It's part of the direction, for him to be trying so desperately to get Mable to agree to run away with him.

"Like what?" I scoff, hands on my hips. I can almost imagine the dress I'll be wearing, the folds of cloth beneath my hands.

Joseph is Trevor again. "Like this."

He kisses me.

That is *so* not in the script.

He grabs the back of my neck, making it difficult to jerk away as fast as I'd like. I manage to squirm free and step back, holding my hands up defensively. "Woah, woah, what the hell?"

Trevor straightens up, still smiling, but a faint frown tugs at his brows. "What? I thought we were having a good moment there."

"We—we were *acting*," I stutter, wiping at my mouth.

"I wasn't."

Shit. What did I do wrong? I rub at my lips again, taking another step back. Even if Trevor thought I was sending some sort of message that I most certainly wasn't, what about, you know, his *girlfriend?* "Why would you do that to Mara?"

His smile fades. "Come on, London. I haven't been happy with Mara in a long time. Don't tell me you didn't notice."

"Could have fooled me. She talks about you like you're the second coming of Christ."

"She's nice and I care about her, but..." He shrugs, running a hand through his hair. "But we aren't compatible in some ways. She's always nagging and she's...kind of a prude."

I stare at him. "A prude."

With a sigh, Trevor begins to pace. "Well, yeah. I mean, we've been dating for months and yet every time we're alone and I try to touch her, she makes me feel guilty for it. Like wanting it is some defect in my brain or something."

"Oh, God forbid a girl not be ready to spread her legs for you," I snap, turning to grab my backpack.

Trevor squares his shoulders and shifts closer like he might try to stop me. "Where are you going?"

"Home." I yank open the bedroom door and stalk out.

Trevor follows. "Come on! It was just a kiss. It doesn't have to be a big deal."

I come to a halt at the top of the stairs and whirl on him, shoving a finger in his face. "It *is* a big deal! I don't care if you're not happy. Mara worships the ground you walk on and if you don't care about her enough to not only respect her decisions but to be faithful to her in the meantime, then I suggest you go play in traffic."

With that, I spin away and jog downstairs and out the door before he can think of something to say.

I hate driving when I'm upset but I'm not about to sit outside Trevor's house and give him the chance to come after me. I drive a few blocks and pull over to give myself a second to calm down.

Mara. God, poor Mara. She's such a sweet girl and all she wants is to see the good in people, so how could someone use her like that? Breaking up with her would crush her, sure, but at least it would leave her free to be with someone who would treat her the way she deserves to be treated. I'm sure Trevor could find plenty of girlfriends who would sleep with him, just like Mara could find a guy who was happy to wait.

I pull my phone out of my pocket and stare at it. She deserves to know about this. How do I tell her? She didn't even know I was coming to Trevor's tonight. Nobody did. Would she believe me if Trevor denied it happened? Me, who she's only been friends with for a few weeks, over the guy she's in love with? I know Trevor will deny it. He gains nothing from being honest.

What would Wade say, I wonder, if he knew his best friend was the kind of guy who would make a move on someone else while in a relationship? I wonder if it would make him think twice about their friendship.

For some reason, I also think about Amber and her reaction. If she would have one. What advice might she give me? She is the only person I put serious consideration into calling but in the end I don't call anyone. I put my phone away, rest my forehead against the steering wheel for a few minutes, and then start the drive home. I have the weekend to think about it. Two days to decide what I'm going to do.

Jasmine's return home on Saturday night is a rather anticlimactic event. Then again, I don't know what I expected. Maybe some happiness. Maybe a sit-down with me, her, and Mom where we all talked about things. None of that happens. Jazz comes in as Mom and I are eating dinner, says, "Hey," and disappears into the bedroom.

Mom finishes up her meal and goes after her. They're in there for a good hour but I don't think it's a conversation I should intrude on. When Mom emerges, her eyes are red from crying and she goes into the kitchen to do the dishes. She doesn't tell me what they talked about, but I'd be lying if I said I didn't want to know. I venture into the bedroom where Jazz is lying on her bed, staring at the ceiling.

"Hi," I say. Jazz makes a noise. I take a seat on my own bed, folding my legs Indian style. "Is everything okay with you and Mom?"

She shrugs. "She asked me not to see Dad anymore."

"What did you say?"

"I told her I couldn't do that." Jazz rolls onto her side to face me. "Would you abandon Mom if she really needed you? Even if she'd fucked up and made some really stupid choices, could you honestly turn your back on her?"

"Mom is different. She's given up a hell of a lot for us. Dad hasn't done anything but use you."

"You make it out like he's some monster who's purposely trying to ruin our lives." Jazz scowls. Did she honestly think I would take her side in this? "I'm a big girl and I can take care of myself. I'm not dragging anyone else into it, so I'd appreciate it if you guys would let me do what I need to do."

I sigh, running my hands over my face. "You don't get it, Jazz. It does affect us. Because it affects you. That medication was *yours* to help *you.* If Dad cared, he couldn't deprive you of something you need for your well-being. You've been a basket-case—"

"Watch it."

"—since you started handing over your pills to him."

"I'm still taking them occasionally."

"That's even worse. You can't pop a pill here and there and expect it not to mess with your brain. It's meant to be taken as the doctor prescribed it. I'm willing to bet you didn't tell Mom that he hit you."

Jasmine responds with nothing more than a steely stare.

"Didn't think so. Did he do it again?"

"No."

"Are you lying to me?"

"I wouldn't tell you even if I were. I can handle myself."

"So you keep saying." When Jazz rolls over and away from me, I relocate to her bed and rub my hand down her back. "Look...I get it. I really, really do. You love Dad and you want him to get better. I'd be ecstatic it if he got himself cleaned up, too. But it has nothing to do with him *wanting* to hurt you or not. He *is* hurting you, and there comes a point in time where you have to look out for yourself before anyone else."

For all of Jazz's self-centeredness, she's a good person. She loves our parents. She wants her family back. She wants her dad to be okay and our mom to be happy. I can't honestly begrudge her that when her intentions are good. However I don't have to enjoy seeing what she has to give up in order to do what she feels she should be doing. Jasmine Noble may bitch and complain and want things her way, but when it comes down to the wire her family comes before her own happiness.

Jazz doesn't respond. Before I draw away, she reaches up and covers my hand with her own and gives it a squeeze. I doubt what I'm saying will change her mind, but I hope she knows I care. I hope she'll at least think about it.

Diary of a Noble

No means no in any language, regardless of gender or social status or relationship status or whatever. Anything other than "yes" is...you guessed it, a no. This goes for sex. This goes for touching, it goes for kissing. I should have kicked him in the teeth for not respecting that. And for not respecting *her*.

Then there's J. I want to shake some sense into her. She's so stubborn and set in her beliefs that I start to wonder if *I'm* the one in the wrong.

What do I do?

I hate that there is so much I can't control.

Come Monday morning, I'm not any closer to knowing what to do about Trevor than I was ten seconds after it happened. I feel like if I were going to tell Mara, I should have called her that night rather than waiting. What if she saw Trevor over the weekend? What if they went out and had a nice date together with her completely unaware? She'll have to reflect back on that if I approach her at school and say anything. I decide my best bet is talking to Wade. He knows Trevor and Mara both well. Maybe he'll have some advice on how I should handle this.

I shove my things into my locker and head to Wade's, hopeful he isn't hanging out with Trevor right now. I find him alone heading down the hall to first period, and jog to catch up.

"Wade!"

There's a pause in his steps, but it's brief. He doesn't stop for me. "I need to get to class, London."

What's with that tone? "Can you hold up for just a sec? We still have ten minutes. I really need to talk to you."

He does stop this time, turning slowly in my direction, but he doesn't look at me. Not really. "I don't feel much like talking right now."

I don't like the tense look on his face. Something isn't right. "What's wrong?"

"Why don't you tell me?"

"Dude, really? If you're pissed at me for something, just say it." I hate the *I'm angry but I won't tell you why* game. Jasmine does it to me all the time.

Wade glances around, shifting his backpack from one shoulder to the other, giving a heavy exhale through his nose. "Why didn't you tell me you went to Trevor's?"

You've got to be kidding me. "I wasn't aware I needed to clear my schedule with you."

"When it involves one of my best friends, I'd kind of like to know. What did you two do?"

"*Do?*" I'm starting to get angry. The way he says it sounds like he's accusing me of planning all this. I set up some super-secret date with Trevor so I could take advantage of him. "He said he wanted help with the play so we were running lines...and he tried to kiss me."

Wade rolls his shoulders into a shrug and glances away. "Yeah, well, that's not what he's saying."

The cold weight of dread descends on my shoulders, making my spine rigid with tension. "What is he saying?"

"That you came on to him." He still won't look at me.

I swallow hard. "And?"

"And...he said you kissed him and talked him into having sex."

A tidal wave of nausea sweeps over me.

Trevor not only took the truth and twisted it, but then embellished it to epic proportions. How could he do this? Not only cheat on Mara but turn around and make it out to be my fault? Not even just a kiss, but he said I *slept with him?* Even if we weren't close, I still considered us sorta-kinda friends. "You can't possibly believe that's true."

Wade finally meets my eyes and I realize...yes, he just might. He thinks I slept with his best friend. "I don't believe you initiated it, but you did say you could be attracted to guys..."

"Attracted doesn't mean I want to fuck them!" A few people passing by glance over at my outburst. I'm bordering on too-upset-to-give-a-shit. "I thought you knew me better than that. A whole lot better. Even if I cared to sleep with a guy, Trevor would not be on the top of my list. How could you think I would do something like that to Mara?"

He looks down, guilt encroaching onto his features. I don't think this is about him believing or not believing me so much as he’s believing Trevor. Snippets of our conversation from the other night replay in my head.

“Oh my god.” Everything makes sense. “The guy you have a crush on is Trevor, isn’t it?”

Wade grimaces. "Keep your voice down."

"You aren't pissed off at the idea that I slept with someone. You're pissed off at the idea *he* did. You know he and Mara aren't having sex so that's fine with you, but..." I can tell by the embarrassed twist of his expression that I'm right. Which only upsets me more. Of course, then, he would believe Trevor over me. Trevor has been his best friend for several years and his crush for who knows how long. Me? I'm just the fake girlfriend who stumbled into his life by accident.

Wade isn’t saying anything. I slowly turn and walk away from him, disappearing into the crowd. I'm done talking. He can be upset all he wants but this isn't something I did. My only mistake was going to Trevor's in the first place.

I spend my day feeling out of sorts. Feeling like people are watching me. It has to be my imagination. I'm dreading that last class of the day where Mara will be seated next to me, because if Wade knows then there's no telling if Trevor fed the same story to Mara.

Before history, though, I'll have to get through lunch. I don't look for any of my drama group where I’ve been sitting the last week or two. Instead I retreat to my usual table outside, despite the cold, and sit down with my bagged lunch and begin nibbling on a sandwich. Two guys who are only vaguely familiar slow when they pass by and they give me grins. One of them says, "Hey, London."

I look up, confused. Trying to place names to faces. I know I've seen them, but they aren’t in any of my classes. "Hi...?"

The boys exchange looks, smirk, and continue on their way. It doesn't occur to me until after they've vanished inside that I do know them from watching Wade and Trevor during swim practice. Allen. That was one of the guys. I didn’t recognize him outside of a swimsuit. So today is coincidentally the day they decide to acknowledge my existence? There goes my appetite. I shove the half-eaten sandwich into the bag. My stomach hurts. I wonder if I could see the school nurse and ask to go home. I'm eighteen, they technically can't stop me.

No. Running away from this isn't going to do me any good. I'll come to school tomorrow and Trevor will still be here. The lie will still be floating around to haunt me. Now that I'm beginning to suspect he told people, I'm also aware that I'm probably not just being paranoid. People *are* watching me. I'm getting looks in the hall like I did when I started “dating” Wade. Except now they aren't curious glances and the occasional annoyed glare. They're hard, judging looks. Because if Trevor is making this lie of his public knowledge, then not only are people who like Mara going to be furious, but all those girls who have a thing for Wade and think I'm his cheating girlfriend are going to tie me to a stake and burn me in the courtyard. I'm not even going to think about what Jazz will say if she catches wind of it.

When the bell for last period rings, I linger in the halls and drag my feet the whole way there. Not only do I have to be in the same room as Mara, but I'll be sitting next to her. In the event I manage to avoid problems there, I still have drama club after school. With Trevor. I'm going to have to pull him aside and confront him no matter how much I don’t want to.

Mara is already seated when I come in. I sit down, studying her from the corner of my eye. She doesn't look at me. If I didn't know better I would say she's putting a lot of effort into keeping her eyes straight ahead.

"Hi Mara."

Mara says, "Don't."

She knows. Or at least, she thinks she knows.

My stomach knots up painfully. I don't want Mara to be upset with me. I need to explain to her. The last bell has rung and Mrs. Scheck is taking her place at the head of the class, but I can't let this go.

"We need to talk after school," I whisper. She stares straight ahead as Mrs. Scheck begins her lecture. I rip a piece of binder paper from a notebook and scribble something down to slip onto Mara's desk. *He's lying.* Mara takes one look at it. The corners of her mouth downturn and she crumples the paper in her hands, tossing it back to my desk.

I slump down, eyes tearing over as I turn my attention to the front of the class. Trevor knew what he was doing. I was right: why would anyone believe me over Trevor, who is well-known and well-liked? I've never cared about people thinking poorly of me before, so long as the reasons were justified. But knowing everyone hates me because of a lie? I can't stand it.

Mara doesn't look at me once throughout the entire class. I struggle to concentrate, but I've never been more grateful to hear the bell ring so I can gather my things and dash out of the room. I need to get to the drama club and talk to Trevor. Get him to straighten all this out.

I beat Mara there, but Wade is already seated on the stage. When I step through the doors he and Trevor stop what they're doing and turn to look at me. Not just them, but several members in other groups, too.

Does everyone know? That can’t be possible. Our school is small, but it’s not *that* small.

Anger bubbles up under my skin. Courage bolstered, I stalk forward. "You son of a bitch."

Trevor holds up his hands. "Look, I'm really sorry, London. I told you what happened was a mistake."

"You're damned right it was a mistake. Who do you think you are?"

"Mara already broke up with me." He frowns. "What more do you want?"

I pause. Is he really going to do this? Pretend *to my face* that his lie is real? "We didn't sleep together and you know it." My voice is rising. Anyone who wasn't paying attention before is definitely paying attention now.

"Are we having a problem over there, buds?" Mr. Cobb calls from across the room. He's normally a quiet, non-entity here in drama, only around to guide us where we need it and serve as a required club chaperone. I want to throw myself at Trevor and punch in his pretty face. Wade won't even look at me. He's staring at his feet.

"Everything's fine," Mara says from behind me. I turn to face her. Her eyes are a bit glassy and she crosses her arms. "London was just leaving."

I am? Is this what it's come to? Everyone sides with Trevor and I get ostracized from the entire club without anyone taking ten seconds to consider my side of things? "Mara..."

"I really, really liked you, London," she says quietly. "I didn't think you were the type of person to do this. Not even to me, but to *Wade.* He doesn't trust people easily and you totally screwed him over."

I turn to Wade, willing him to just...look at me. I could spill our secret right here and now. I could tell Mara that I'm gay. I could tell her there's no possible way I would have slept with Trevor because I like *her*. And I would. I would in a heartbeat just to see the look on Trevor's face.

But I can't, because I wouldn't be the only one in the spotlight then. Everyone would look at Wade and wonder why he would date a lesbian. Either he knew and acted as a cover (why, unless he also had something to hide?) or he didn't know and I still look like the bad guy for leading him on.

There is nothing I can do if no one will believe me.

The room is deadly silent. Even the sound of my breathing is too loud. I tighten my grip on my backpack strap and without a word step around Mara to head for the door. Just like that. One little mistake because I was trying to help someone out, and I've been shoved aside. The moment I hit the threshold people begin to whisper. Maybe about me. Probably about me.

Outside, I run into Amber. She seems to have been waiting there for me rather than risk walking into the battlefield of the drama room. I stop a few feet away, struggling to bite back my tears. Her head tilts to one side, expression unreadable.

"No," I manage, and despite my efforts the tears are slipping down my face and my voices cracks and wobbles. "I didn't sleep with him. I didn't sleep with anyone. No one believes me."

"They wouldn't," she says mildly. "Everyone loves Trevor. No one even knew your name until you started dating Wade."

I wonder if this means Amber believes him, too. My head ducks and I hug myself, feeling sick with the weight of all this.

Amber takes a step closer and brings her hands to my face, wiping the tears from my cheeks with her thumbs. Her hands are soft. They smell of soap and paint. I look up and meet her eyes with only a few inches separating us, and I wish I could get my throat to work so I could tell her how much it would mean if she would stick by me. If I had one person that understood, that knows like I do that this is only going to get worse now that I've been publically humiliated by both Mara and Trevor. Wade, too, with the way he so blatantly turned his back on me.

Amber opens her mouth, seems to think better of whatever she was going to say, and draws back with a shake of her head. She steps around me and goes into the drama room, leaving me alone.

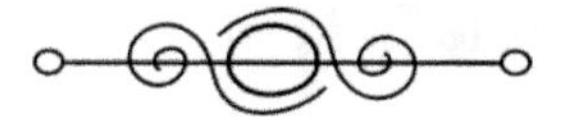

Jazz is already home when I come into the apartment. She must have gotten a ride from a friend or Dad because the bus wouldn't have been so fast. I don't want to see her. I don't want to know if she heard what was being said, and more than that I don't want to be screamed at. I wish Mom were home.

My sister looks up at me from the couch, lips pursed. Maybe she takes note of my tear-streaked face or my red eyes, because even as I'm briskly moving across the living room she is getting up to follow me.

"London?"

"Don't," I mutter, vanishing into the bathroom. It's the only place I can go wherein I can lock the door, turn on the water, and try to drown everything out for a bit. Jazz knocks on the door and her voice is surprisingly soft.

"Lonny. Let me in. Are you okay?"

Jasmine hasn't called me that in ages. She isn't screaming but the concern in her voice tells me she probably knows. I'm not sure what to make of that, but I reluctantly unlock the door. Jazz eases it open and slips inside, taking a seat on the edge of the tub to face me sitting on the closed toilet lid.

"Are you here to yell at me?"

"No. I'm still trying to figure out if I believe it or not."

I rub at my eyes. “What makes you think it isn’t true?”

Jasmine shrugs. “Because it's not you. I mean, yeah, you've been acting weird lately, getting all into drama again and dating Wade or whatever, but I know you. You've never cheated on a test, let alone a person. You have the most ridiculous guilty conscience. So...I don’t know. I’m finding it hard to believe."

That's true, but I haven't known my friends (ex-friends?) long enough for them to know that. I lift my puffy eyes to Jazz's face and wonder if I should tell her that I was never really dating Wade. I don't, because this is the first time in as long as I can remember that Jazz has spoken so gently and kindly to me, and I don't want to do anything to make her stop. I need someone to understand, even if it doesn't make a difference in the grand scheme of things. Maybe she doesn’t fully believe me, but there’s a chance and I'll take whatever I can get.

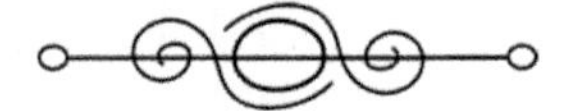

Diary of a Noble

Maybe I should have stayed a Nobody.

19

Tuesday morning, I manage to get out of bed and go to school only because Jazz prods me into it. I tell myself: today will be better. Things will have died down and that maybe after a few days Mara will have calmed enough that I can talk sense into her. I've decided even if they've effectively kicked me out of drama, I'm going to finish up the costumes and deliver them. Just because Trevor is a dick doesn't mean I'm going to leave the group high and dry when it comes to their (our?) play.

Surprisingly Jazz sticks by me as we get out of the car and head toward school, but I can tell she's uncomfortable. Being seen with me right now would be even worse and I'm touched she'd bother trying at all.

"Go on," I tell her at the edge of the parking lot. "I'll be fine." She gratefully jogs off toward the building. I give her enough time to undoubtedly locate some of her friends before heading inside. I swing by my locker to deposit my books and pause when I see a folded up piece of paper someone slipped through the slots in my locker door. My insides flip-flops as I open it.

Whore

Lovely. I swallow hard and crumple up the page. I doubt it's from anyone I know, and that almost—*almost*—makes it worse. I'm not about to let it ruin my day. I can't expect everyone to have forgotten about it twenty-four hours later, after all. I pitch the wad of paper into the nearest trashcan and head to class.

Strike number two comes in the form of swim team Allen taking it upon himself to smack my ass in the hall between second and third period. I whirl around and punch him in the arm so fast that his yelp draws more attention than the initial ass-smacking did.

"What the *hell*?" I snarl.

"That hurt." He rubs his arm. "I didn't do anything!"

"You touched my ass, douchebag!"

He lets out a loud, barking laugh. "Yeah, right. I'm not touching anything that's been around as much as you have." He bares his teeth in a shit-eating grin and strolls off through the crowd, leaving me with a sinking feeling about what he meant by that.

Strike three elaborates on that thought. One of Missy's friends manages a not very subtle "Slut," on my way to Mrs. Scheck's class. Her friends—Missy included—snicker and giggle behind their hands, and it's all I can do to keep my gaze straight ahead and not respond. It isn't worth getting into a fight over. Especially not one where I'd be severely outnumbered.

Mara has nothing to say to me in class and I don't push my luck trying to talk to her. She's out the door the second the bell rings. I find myself at a loss. I can't go to drama. I've grown used to being there, to having friends, to not going straight home to do absolutely nothing.

It hurts.

Jazz is waiting for me by the car. I thought she had plans to go see Dad tonight, but she shrugs it off when I ask and suggests we pick up dinner. Together. Like, doing sisterly things. I really do think she's lost her mind. Either that or she feels sorry for me. No complaints here. We pick up some burgers, fries, and milkshakes—the dinner of champions, right?—and park our butts on the couch to watch TV while we eat in silence. It's okay that we aren't talking. I appreciate her nearness more than I can say.

No sooner have we finished eating, though, than her phone is ringing and she's slipping into the kitchen to answer it. Meaning, it must be Dad. She emerges a few minutes later, frowning.

"Sorry. Dad's having a rough night, so I'm gonna grab a cup of coffee with him." She's already slipping her shoes and jacket back on.

I try not to look as disappointed as I feel. The last thing I want is to be left alone for hours, and Mom isn't scheduled home until after I'm likely to be asleep. I don't feel like going out anywhere, either.

My sullenness makes me mutter, "What, does he need more pills?"

Jazz shoots me a look. "I don't have anything to give him."

"Does he know that?"

I'm rewarded only with a snort and a "see you later" as she disappears out the front door to go downstairs and wait for Dad.

I finish off my fries and try calling Trevor. Not because I want to talk to him, exactly, but because I figure talking to him with no one else around will yield better results. When he doesn't answer, I don't bother leaving a message and instead station myself at the dining table to get my homework done. I have to admit, my attention to it has dwindled a little in that past several weeks since I got a semi-social life. Not enough to affect my grades, thankfully.

My phone rings just as I'm starting on calculus equations and the sound is startling and worrying all at once. Especially when I see Amber's name pop up on the screen. I stare at my phone vibrating across the table for four or five rings before I pick it up and answer. "Hello...?"

"Hey."

"Hi." Pause. "Uh. What's up...?"

Amber sighs. "I sort of thought I should warn you before you go to school tomorrow."

Well, that sounds awesome. "Warn me about what?"

"This thing with Trevor is kind of blowing up. Some of his friends have jumped on board. They're saying they slept with you, too."

Good thing I'm already sitting down. I don't feel well. "I...don't understand. What are they getting out of this? They don't even *know* me."

"I couldn't say. Maybe Trevor talked them into it. Or maybe they think it'll make them look good, adding another name to their lists or something."

I press the heel of my hand against my forehead. This spark is turning into a forest fire, and I have no idea how to put it out. "Fuck me. I need to talk to Trevor."

"Don't, London. It'll only make things worse. He'll play it off like you're obsessing over him."

As much as I'd like to think Trevor isn't that much of an ass, he's sort of proven he can and will stoop that low, and everyone will fall for it. "So...what? I suck it up and pretend nothing's wrong, then?"

"I don't know how to answer that. Try to keep your head down. People will hang onto this because it's new gossip. They'll get bored with it when something else comes along. Look, I gotta go. I just wanted to give you a heads up."

"I appreciate it. Thanks."

Amber says goodnight and hangs up. I place my phone on the table and rest my chin in my hands, eyes closed. So her suggestion is for me to fade back into obscurity? I tried so hard to get to where I am, to be normal. Mom will be disappointed when I tell her I'm not going to be in a play after all.

Which reminds me: once I've finished with my homework, I drag out my sewing machine and the unfinished costumes. I have half a mind to make the stitching on Trevor's loose. I hope it splits in the middle of his monologue.

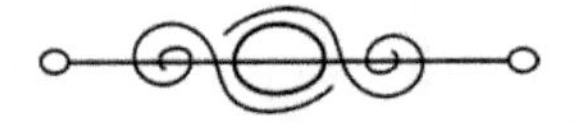

Diary of a Noble

Three costumes, all complete. I wonder who they'll get to play my part. I was honestly really looking forward to it. I wanted to make Mom proud.

20

I try to follow Amber's advice. Keep my head down. Don't react to anything anyone says. I get a few more notes shoved in my locker. I've taken to not opening them. See paper? Throw paper in trash.

By Thursday I've finished the costumes. I fold them neatly and bring them to school in a paper bag. I didn't see the point of finishing Mable's, really, but I made it anyway. It should fit Amber if they can talk her into taking my role. Otherwise, maybe Wade will rewrite the entire play. Who knows?

I tuck the bag safely into my locker where I can retrieve it closer to last period and when I turn around, I spot Trevor at the far end of the hall. Alone. None of his friends. No Wade. No Mara. Amber told me not to confront him but I can't help it. He's *right there* and I want to hear from his own mouth why he did this to me.

"Trevor."

He stops walking and pivots to look at me, eyebrows raised like he's amazed I had the audacity to approach him. "Hey, London. I don't really have time to talk right now."

"You can talk or I'm knocking your teeth out," I say icily. "You at least owe me an explanation."

Trevor holds out his hands in a helpless gesture. "You were going to tell Mara that I made a move on you. The only way for me to avoid it was to do it first."

"What's the point? She still broke up with you."

"Yeah, but no one else gives a shit. *You* took advantage of *me*. You have any idea how many girls have slipped me their number in the last few days?"

I stare at him. Really stare at him. He isn't smiling but I can tell what he's saying is the entire truth. He's dragging me through the mud just so he doesn't look like a complete and utter dick. Somehow, someway, he has spun this entire situation to paint him out as the victim.

"I knew you were kind of an ass, Trevor, but I didn't think you were this kind of person."

"For what it's worth, I didn't mean for it to turn into this big thing." He almost looks sorry. "I didn't tell any of my friends to say anything. They did that on their own."

"I haven't slept with any of them, either!"

He shrugs again. "They're all grown boys. Sorry, but I can't control them. See you around." He turns away and I don't know what else to say to him. Frankly, I want to throw myself at his retreating back and beat his face into the ground.

This is what people are capable of doing to others.

What a sad, sad world.

Today is going to be one of those days. I keep my chin up and I go to class, refusing to meet anyone's gaze. Let them stare. Let them talk. Let them think they know a damned thing about me and waste their time trying to drag me down. I will not let it happen.

I had planned on giving the costumes to Mara at the end of the day, but I spot Amber between classes after lunch first and thankfully she doesn't ignore me when I wave her down. She might be the only person in this entire school who isn't giggling at me behind my back or avoiding me all together.

"I have the outfits," I say. "For the play."

Amber blinks. "You finished them?"

"You guys need costumes, don't you?" I give a one shouldered shrug and lead her back to my locker. "You're still doing it, right?"

"Hopefully. Mara's trying to talk me into playing Mable." She doesn't sound pleased by this and I don't blame her. Amber went into this wanting to design sets, not act. Especially asking her to play someone as exuberant and out there as Mable, I can understand her reluctance.

"It could be fun. Wade can always try to tone the character down, or maybe you could switch with Mara and play Anna instead."

Amber starts to say something and stops. She grabs my arm tightly and drags me to face her. "You know what, let's get the costumes later. I don't want to be late for class."

"What? My locker is right there—" When I look over my shoulder, I see exactly what Amber hadn't wanted me to see.

I twist free from her grasp and approach my locker. Plastered all over the door are sanitary pads. Each one is labeled with a different word in red lipstick. *Slut. Whore. Tramp.* And, right there in the middle, *Dirty London.*

My eyes well with tears. I burst into laughter.

It's *so fucking ridiculous* and overdramatic and reeks of high school immaturity. This is not my life. This is an idiotic teen TV show. I can't stand it. Amber rushes to my side and wraps an arm around me, drawing me to her, and I bury my face against her shoulder while I laugh and sob like I've lost my mind. I hear her using her free hand to rip the pads off my locker while she murmurs softly to me, "Shh, shh, it's okay. They're stupid. They're all stupid..."

I don't look up because I don't want to know who is watching. Amber is leading me, I'm not sure where. Too busy keeping my head down, my eyes closed. At least until she gets me into the bathroom where it's quiet and I dare to look up and pull away, wiping at my tears.

Amber shadows my every movement as I step over to the sink. I see her worried reflection in the mirror. "God, London, I'm so sorry..."

I twist the tap to get cold water going. "It's funny, isn't it? I spent years avoiding all this kind of shit and the one time I try to fit in..." I shake my head and cup water in my hands to splash it on my face. "You shouldn't be here. They'll probably start saying you slept with half the swim team, too."

"I'm not worried about it." Amber grabs me a few paper towels as I lean back against the sink. I dry my hands off and chuck the waded up tissue into the trash. "Trevor is an asshole and as long as he sees that it bothers you, he'll keep it up. He gets a kick out of it."

I sniff and give one last swipe at my burning eyes. "How do you know?"

"Because I've been where you are." Amber takes a deep breath and crosses her arms. "He did the same thing to me in freshman year."

That's enough to snap me out of my self-pity. My gaze lifts to her face. "What?"

She shrugs, studying her feet. "We were lab partners. He wanted me to come over to study. Said he needed help. It was going to affect my grade, too, so I agreed."

Sounds all too familiar. Too familiar for comfort, in fact.

"Halfway through the assignment, he started telling me how pretty I was. He kept...playing with my hair and leaning in real close." She hugs herself tighter. "Then he kissed me. And at first I thought...maybe it was okay because we were both single and I liked him, but he kept pushing it. He wouldn't stop when I asked him to. He just...pushed me down onto the floor and climbed on top of me and kept kissing."

My heart is about to drop right out of me. "Amber, did he—"

"No," she says quickly. "No. I fought and he finally let me up so it's not like it got that far, but I kept feeling like..."

"Like he could have."

"Yeah." Her shoulders rise and fall in a helpless shrug. "The next day at school, he told everyone that we had had sex. I think I blamed myself for a long time because it's not like I immediately told him no."

"It doesn't matter," I say hotly. "No means no."

"I get that *now*, but it took a long while." Her eyes are glassy. She isn't crying, not exactly, but I can tell it's taking effort. "No one believed me so it was easier to kind of fade into the crowd."

"How can you even stand to be around him anymore?"

"It's not like don't I try. But by avoiding him, I figured I was letting him win. We've had classes together. Then in drama club, Mara became my friend and where Mara went...well, there he was."

I wonder if she's told this to anyone or if she's suffered quietly the last few years, struggling to figure out if it was something she'd done. I can only imagine how scary that must have been, to be overpowered and held against your will by someone bigger and stronger than you.

I hug her without thinking about it. Just...gather Amber into my arms and squeeze her tight, and it's as much for me as it is for her. She unfolds from herself and wraps around me instead. Her fingers dig into my back, her face against my neck. I don't want to think about someone hurting her this way. Someone changing who she is all because...what? Because Trevor wanted to get laid?

"It's not your fault," I mumble.

Amber replies, "It's not your fault, either."

We both know, on a logical level. Maybe our hearts need a bit of convincing.

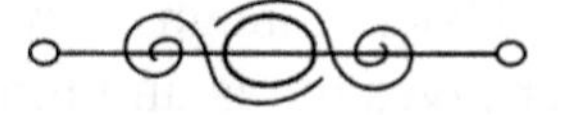

Amber comes home with me after school. She sits cross-legged on my bed while she pulls the costumes out of the bag, smiling. "These are awesome."

I shrug. "I didn't mean to rush so much at the end, but I hope they'll work."

"They're perfect, London. I doubt any of the other groups will have costumes like this."

"Home-made? No. They probably had their parents buy theirs." I grin. Amber laughs, folds up Anna's dress and tucks it carefully away. It makes me wonder, "How is Mara handling this whole thing? I mean, still being in the group with him and all?"

"She's pissed at him, but...you know Mara. She's good at being civil even when she doesn't want to."

"I couldn't tell. She hasn't said a word to me."

"It's a lot for her to take in, I think. Wade and I have talked to her so it should just be a matter of time before she eases up and tries to talk to you."

Wait—"Wade talked to her?"

"Well, yeah. Why wouldn't he?"

"Because *he* hasn't been talking to me, either." Granted, I did kind of chew him out because he was acting like a jerk and Wade is great at retreating from conflict. Maybe he thinks I'm still pissed at him. I sort of am. Maybe not so much pissed as hurt that he didn't even stop to hear my side of things before condemning me.

"He's been pretty bummed out lately." Amber's gaze wanders the bedroom. "I'm sure you two will work things out and get back together."

Get back—oh. "Yeah. Maybe."

She brings her gaze full circle to regard me with one thin eyebrow arched. "You're horrible at sounding convincing when it comes to him. You know that, right?"

I try to look busy by picking lint off my comforter. "I don't know what you're talking about."

"I'm talking about how your relationship with Wade is as real as a three dollar bill."

My shoulders roll back. I laugh, nervously. "*What*?"

The look Amber gives me is an unimpressed one. "I really hope it's fake, because there is nothing about the vibe you two give off together that screams intimacy."

Heat washes up into my face. "Rude."

"Yet completely true." She picks herself up off the bed, crossing her arms and coming to stand in front of me. "Though what I haven't figured out is *why?*"

I stare up at Amber, blushing from head to toe. She has part of the equation figured out and I'm actually okay with that, but what reasoning can I give her without spilling the whole truth? "In all your thinking, have you come up with any guesses?"

"A few. Like, maybe one of you was blackmailing the other for some reason. Again, why?"

"Not even close. But that's funny."

"Hm." Amber purses her lips. She has this way of looking down at me, her eyes half-lidded, that nearly has me squirming with its intensity. Not in a bad way, just a...very Amber way.

"Maybe one of you had a secret to hide, then. Something that would be covered up by dating."

My bottom lip has found its way into my mouth and I chew it viciously. Shoving a pair of scissors into my hammering heart would be less painful than this anticipation. Does she have it worked out or not? And if she does, could I admit to it? Amber is the only person who has stuck by my side through this, the only friend I still have. The thought of her finding out I'm gay makes every horrible possible reaction she could have swim behind my eyes.

I want her to know in every single way that I don't want her to know at the same time. Just for that one percent chance she won't care. "What kind of secret?"

Amber leans down until her face is only few inches from mine, like she can see into my head by doing so. The faint scent of lavender clings to her hair. My pulse flutters and, oh, god, I'm staring at her mouth and wondering what it might be like to—

The thought is gone as quickly as it appeared. Amber leans away and I'm left almost dazed from having her in my personal space like that. I've never thought of Amber in anything more than a platonic sense...have I? However the way she's standing there, hips cocked, head tilted, makes me question it.

After a moment, the answer she comes up with is, "If I told you, it wouldn't be much of a secret, would it?"

I swallow hard. "I guess not."

"You and your secrets..." Amber turns away. She's silent a moment, then reaches out to pick up a picture frame on my bedside table next to the lamp. The same picture of me and Jazz that Wade saw when he was in my room. I can't see her face, but her shoulders seem to slump the slightest bit. I wonder what she thinks of the old me, with the platinum blonde hair and bubblegum-colored streaks and rainbow clothes.

"What is it?" I ask now that I can breathe properly again.

Amber murmurs, "This was you."

"It *is* me."

"Was," she corrects quietly. "You should go back to this."

I frown deeply, pushing to my feet to step up beside her and peer into the picture. I remember the exact moment it was taken. It was the summer before I started high school. Jazz and I were sharing ice cream on Pier 39 in San Francisco, one of the very few trips Mom was ever able to take us on. We went to the aquarium, took photos of Alcatraz from afar since we couldn't afford to actually go, and ate at Bubba Gump Shrimp for lunch. If I really think on it, it might have been the last time we felt like a real, legitimate family.

"I can't just go back to it." I take the photo from her hands and returning it to its proper place. "What does an outfit and a box of hair dye change about anything?"

“It’s not the things you wore and your hair, London.” She shakes her head. “It’s the way you’re standing, it’s the look on your face. You were confident and didn’t care what other people thought.”

“You told me I should keep my head down."

Amber lifts her chin. There is something distant and sad in the depths of her eyes. "I think I was wrong."

That gives me pause. "Why?"

"Because hiding and pretending it didn't happen is what I did. Do I look happy to you? I kept thinking by not letting Trevor know how devastated and scared I was, I kept him from winning. Instead it just taught him it was okay to put others through the same thing. He's happy, and I'm not."

I don't know what to say to that beyond, "You can't blame yourself for his actions."

"I'm blaming myself for *my* actions, London." She shakes her head, swiping at her eyes. "Here I am telling you to do the exact same thing when I should be encouraging you to do whatever you want to do. So long as you're being yourself." Before I can say anything, she holds up a hand. "I don't mean the hair and the clothes, I just mean...*you*. Don't keep secrets about who you are, even if others won't understand. Don't sit quietly when you want to be heard. You were—*are*—beautiful. Don't hide that."

My eyes are locked onto Amber, unsure of how to respond. When we met, I saw a quiet, sullen girl who found interaction a nuisance. Now, I'm looking at someone who spent her first few high school years being alone and frightened, always questioning the motives of others, and who thought it best to hold everyone at bay so she could keep her heart from being broken. She wanted to protect me from what she dealt with, and perhaps she's realizing that she can't.

Without thinking twice, I take Amber's hand in my own until she looks at me, a tear threatening to escape down her cheek. I thumb it away for her.

"You're one to talk," I say gently. "I have an idea. If I'm going to do it, though, you have to do it with me."

21

From the Blog of Dirty London

A single moment can change everything you thought you knew.

I thought Mom, Dad, J and I would always be a family. I thought J would always be my baby sister who crawled into bed with me when she had nightmares and who asked me for help with her homework. I thought I would always be Daddy's little girl. His baby London. He'd never miss one of my plays for all the world. He'd have my hand when I walked down the aisle—no matter if it was to give me away to a man or a woman—and, hell, maybe someday he'd hold a grandchild or two. He and Mom would always be in love. They would always be safe and happy.

Reality hurts and breaks and shreds so many dreams and sometimes makes you wonder what it's all for. If your family falls apart and the people you thought would be in your life forever have abandoned you, what good is faith? I have spent so much time hiding these last few years that I think I had forgotten what it was like to have real, tangible hope that things could work out. I was always waiting for the worst to be over before lifting my head from the sand, and in doing so, I've missed so much.

I think I forgot that I deserve to be happy. Not just me, but A, too. We are two diamonds hidden in the dirt. Somewhere along the way, in trying not to get hurt, we buried everything we used to love about ourselves instead of embracing our beauty and what others have labeled our flaws.

Let's get back to that, shall we?

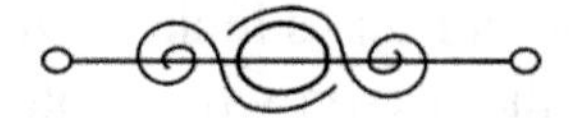

Mom is downing a cup of coffee in preparation for work when I emerge from my room Friday morning. She takes one look at my freshly bleached hair and the fact I'm not wearing the school uniform like I always do, even on casual Fridays, and slowly lowers her mug. I grab a bagel from the cupboard and hold it between my teeth while slipping into my jacket. It feels so strange to be in these clothes. Black boots and leggings and denim shorts with a band t-shirt. It isn't my Rainbow Brite phase from seventh grade, but it doesn't need to be. It just needs to be *me.*

The bagel is crammed into my coat pocket. I shoulder my backpack and lean up to kiss Mom on the cheek. "I've gotta run."

"London?"

I glance back. "Hm?"

Mom smiles. "You look beautiful."

A grin spreads across my face. Three little words and I'm able to straighten my spine and hold my head a little higher. Confidence is good. I'm going to need it today. I'd be lying if I said I wasn't terrified to walk across that parking lot and into school. Everyone in our small uppity school knows my name now and there are eyes on me as my boots echo on the linoleum heading to my locker.

The moment I open the door, I know someone has left me a present. Great. Inside is a pair of underwear with a note attached: *'U left these at my place last night*.' I feel my stomach twist, my throat close. I can't let them get to me anymore. I can't keep my head down and I can't play the victim. Not just for me, but for Amber. I need to be strong for her.

"What's this?" I turn around to face the others mingling in the hall. Whoever put these here is likely hanging around to see my reaction. I hold the underwear out for all to see, letting them dangle from a finger while I open the note with my other hand. "*'I thought these would look nice on you*'?"

"That's not what it says," someone blurts.

I look up, right into the face of Allen Hecklin leaning against the row of lockers across from me with his friends. I wonder if his girlfriend Missy would find it funny that he's sticking panties into another girl's locker. Of course that's not what the note says and only the person who wrote it would know. Allen seems to realize this the moment the words leave his mouth. His face burns red.

"You can give these back to your mom." I throw the underwear at his feet, slam the locker door, and walk away.

Stepping into that drama room is going to be the hardest part of the day. I can shrug off the opinions of people I hardly know, but this is Mara and Wade we're talking about, not to mention I'll be facing down Trevor. Nothing has technically changed. It's still my word against his, and my word isn't worth much.

I push the door open and stroll in with my head held high and my shoulders back. Mara saw me once today so my appearance doesn't throw her off, but she does a double take at the sight of me anyway. Because I'm *here*, and everyone knows I shouldn't be.

Except for Amber. She brings her script to her face to hide her smile, but I see the crinkle around her eyes. Just as we agreed, she has her hair down but out of her face, and she's traded in her baggy pants and sweaters for an outfit we picked out together at the mall after school yesterday: a knit sweater and leggings with shoes to match; an ensemble she had admired many times but never had the courage to wear lest she draw attention. I'm actually glad she kept the glasses. She looks adorable in them.

This was our agreement. Getting back to ourselves.

"Hello, ladies," I greet, coming to a halt in front of where they're seated on the edge of the stage and dropping my back pack. "Where are the boys?"

Mara doesn't look...angry, exactly, just confused. She is still grasping for words when Trevor and Wade come into the theater. There's a hitch in Wade's steps, a brief flicker of surprise, and then he smiles. I've missed that smile. I have to resist the urge to run up and hug him.

Trevor never gets over the shock and his frown is less than friendly. "What are you doing, London?"

"I came to rehearse, of course."

"You aren't in the group anymore."

"Oh. I'm not?" I fold my arms, turning to face him fully. My boots give me a solid inch and a half of height and Trevor isn't particularly tall to begin with, which means I'm close to being eye level with him now. Maybe I've learned a few things from Jasmine, like how to look down on someone even when they're taller than you. "Because you said so? Are you in charge here, Trevor?"

His jaw tenses. "No. Because no one wants you here."

"I do," Amber drawls.

Before Trevor can respond, Wade adds softly, "I do, too."

Wade's support is a pleasant surprise. I smile. "That's two against one."

Trevor takes a deep breath, forces his mouth to upturn, and looks past me. "What about you, Mara? Do you want London here?"

I turn to look at her. Mara, who I've adored from a distance for ages now. Who welcomed me into this group with open arms and trusted me with such an important role. Yet I'm not sure I see her the same anymore. Not after she was so quick to believe Trevor and turn her back on me. To a point, I can understand the loyalty. But if she would believe Trevor could cheat on her, why couldn't she believe he'd lie about it? Only Trevor had something to lose by telling the truth.

Mara crosses her arms, expression guarded. "We kind of need her," she admits. "Amber won't play Mable, and London went through all the trouble to make those costumes even when she didn't have to."

Trevor groans. "This is bull shit."

"Having you in the group is bull shit, too," Amber says tersely.

"I already have to be civil to you," Mara tells Trevor. "There's no reason I can't work with London, too. This play is all of ours, and we should all get to finish it."

"So you're cool with having the girl that slept with me—"

"Oh, *please.*" Amber climbs up on the stage, peering down at all of us. "She didn't sleep with you anymore than I slept with you in freshman year."

Trevor goes still, regarding her with wide eyes that clearly say he wasn't expecting that. I almost wonder if he'd forgotten about it until now. I wouldn't be surprised.

Mara frowns, looking up at Amber. "You didn't...?"

"No." Amber inclines her chin, steely gaze on Trevor. I can hear the waver in her voice, the uncertainty, but she keeps on. "He wanted to. I said no. He didn't like that, so the next day at school he went ahead and told his friends I put out. Same thing he did with London."

"She's lying." Trevor balls his hands into fists. Mara stares at him with a wounded look that about breaks my heart, like she doesn't know what to believe. How it must feel, I wonder, to find out the person you've loved and devoted yourself to is a complete and utter bag of dicks. In front of an auditorium of people, even. There are no less than twenty other students watching our drama spill all over the theater.

"I'm staying," I say to Trevor. "If you don't like it, you're free to leave. The door is over there."

His face reddens. This isn't going his way, not at all. I'm aware it likely has nothing to do with the play itself. Trevor has never cared much about it; he was here at Mara's behest and he has stuck around, perhaps, in hopes of winning back her favor. She was his mountain to climb, and he hadn't been ready to give up until...what, until he conquered her? I don't know. I can't pretend to understand what he's thinking. Maybe in his own twisted way, he does care about her.

Trevor stalks toward me and although I doubt he's going to do anything other than get in my face, I picture him with Amber. Pinning her down, trying to hold her still. I can't help it. I flinch back, shoulders tense, posture ready to lash out if he so much as thinks about touching me.

Not that he gets the chance. Wade catches Trevor by the bicep. His voice is calm and low, but warning. "Not worth it, man. Leave it alone."

Trevor wrenches his arm away. "Don't touch me, you fucking fag!"

Wade's face blanches. His grip goes slack. Trevor is out the door while the entire room is struck into dumb silence, and every pair of eyes is on Wade.

It could have been a simple insult by an idiot. I don't know how it looks from an outsider's perspective. Are people smart enough to take that insult and put two and two together? Wade's lack of girlfriends. His disinterest in dating or sex, and the way he's been attached to Trevor's hip for the better part of his high school life.

Wade looks about three seconds from screaming or crying. He stoops to gather his backpack, painfully slow as though the entirety of the student body will lunge for him if he makes any sudden movements.

"Wade," I whisper, stepping closer.

He backs away, shakes his head, and retreats from the auditorium without a word. I don't know if I should go after him or not. A look behind me shows Amber with her eyes downcast, and Mara with a hand over her mouth. Mara meets my gaze, her worried brows drawn together.

"Why would Trevor say that...?"

The question makes me want to shake her. "Does it matter? Does it really, honestly matter?" Because she's sweet, polite Mara, she blushes and has the grace to look guilty. But it's enough. If even Mara balks at something like this, then what is the rest of the school going to say?

I grab my backpack and hurry after Wade. I catch sight of him just before he disappears into the boys' bathroom. Groaning, I stop just outside.

"Wade, I know you're in there. Will you come out and talk to me? Please?"

No answer. Great.

I glance around to ensure the coast is clear before slipping inside. Good thing no one is really here, given the after school hours. I find him hunched over a sink, hands braced on the edge, water running.

"Wade?"

He jerks upright, running a hand down his wet face. "Jesus, London. You can't come in here!"

"I can, and I did." I cram my hands into my pockets and shrug. What is the worst that can happen? Someone walks in and kicks me out? Would not be the worst thing to happen to me this year. "Are you all right?"

As though the answer isn't obvious. I'm not sure if he's been crying or if he's just been splashing water on his face, but he looks spooked. Not upset so much as frightened.

"I'm fine," he replies, voice tight. "Nothing's going to come of it, I guess it just...scared me a little."

Something could come of it and we both know it, but I can't bring myself to shove that in his face. "Why would he even say something like that?"

Wade looks at the floor. My eyes widen.

"Wait, you *told him?*"

"Yes. No. I don't know." He turns off the sink and rubs the back of his neck with a sigh. "I think I sort of...I might have...hit on him?"

Yuck. "You...hit on him."

"Yes," he groans. "I hit on him, all right? Sort of."

"How did you sort of hit on Trevor?"

"I went over to his place last night after practice. I think I just...eluded to the idea that there were plenty of girls out there besides Mara...and some guys." Wade grimaces at the memory. I wonder how hard he wanted to punch himself after those words fell out of his mouth. "He got real quiet and kept giving me these weird looks, so I left. He was fine this morning, so I thought..."

I move over beside him and take his damp hands in mine. "Can I ask something without seeming like a jerk?"

He sighs. "Go ahead."

"What do you even see in him?"

Wade studies our joined hands. "What did you think of him before all this happened?"

I open my mouth and then pause. Oh. "I thought he was a nice guy."

"Exactly. Trevor is likeable. He's funny and he's up for anything. I can't count the number of times he's come to my rescue to help me practice for a competition or fill out college applications. Nobody gave a shit about me until Trevor took me under his wing." Wade shakes his head. "The Trevor I knew—*thought* I knew—was a little temperamental and had a big mouth but he was fun. He wasn't bad."

It's no different than Mara. She thought she knew Trevor, too. Maybe they do. Maybe Trevor is not an inherently bad person, just a person who has made some really shitty decisions. If it were only what he had done to me in question, I might even forgive him, but...

"I can't overlook what he did to you or Amber," I say. "I'm sorry."

Wade doesn't lift his head. He traces his thumbs over my knuckles, one at a time, his mouth downturned and brows knitted together in a worried frown. "Everyone is going to know about this by tomorrow."

"They're going to know Trevor made an idiot out of himself. That's all." I give his hands a squeeze. "Everything is going to be all right." I hug him as though to prove this point. Wade bows down, pressing his face against my shoulder and holding me tight, like I might somehow shield him from all of this. I wish that I could.

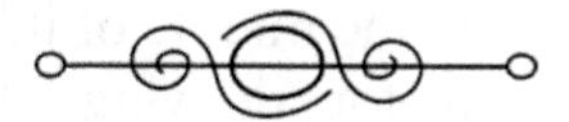

Day one of 'finding myself' didn't go too badly, all things considered. I'm back in the play. Wade and I are speaking again, and even Mara seems to have made peace with what happened. Sort of. If not, then she's damned good at faking it. As for me... Maybe my comfortable clothes and the few compliments I got on my hair helped to drown out the rumors going around. Just because the drama club saw Trevor take a nosedive into the liar-liar pool doesn't mean everyone else in the school knows yet. Or that they'll believe it. I'm still the slut who slept my way around the swim team.

The after school plan had originally been for me to drop Jasmine off at Dad's house. Not because I want to, but because the sky is threatening rain and I don't want her out in it. When we get into the car after school she says, "I'm just going home today."

I look at her askance and start up the car. "Okay. Dad have plans or something?"

She shrugs and looks out the window.

If I had to guess what her problem is, I would say it's that since she hasn't had any medication to give him, Dad hasn't been interested in keeping Jazz around as much. Last night, she went to visit and was gone barely an hour before she came shuffling home, quiet and crestfallen. Now would not be the best time to say *I told you so.* I'll settle for gently patting her leg before pulling out of the parking lot.

She's silent the whole trip home. It isn't until we reach the apartment and have dragged our backpacks into the bedroom that Jazz idly comments, "I heard Trevor and Wade got into a fight during drama."

Well, there goes my theory that no one would find out. Jazz has friends all over school; I'm sure some of them are in after school clubs. "Inaccurate. It was more like me, Mara, and Amber against Trevor."

Mildly interested, Jazz watches me from the corner of her gaze as she digs her text books from her backpack. "What happened?"

"I called him out for being a lying douchebag. With a little help. Wade got dragged into the middle of it."

"You're on a roll for drawing attention." The sullen undertone to her voice does not go unnoticed.

I sink onto my bed, pulling my history book out. "I'm trying to be myself, that's all. You got a problem with it?"

Jasmine's face twists into a bit of a pout. "Whatever. It just doesn't exactly make my life easy."

The effort it takes not to throw something at her is astounding. "Sorry, I forgot my role in the grand plan of the universe is to make your social life a little more convenient."

Instead of me throwing something at her, though, Jasmine picks up a pillow and chucks it in my direction. I manage to catch it before it smacks me in the face. She snaps, "You think it's funny and it's really not! I've had to deal with people asking me about all these stupid rumors too, you know."

I toss the pillow to the floor, determined not to be ruffled by this. Today was so draining and I don't want to be upset with her on top of it all. "Let it go, Jasmine. They aren't true. You said so yourself you didn't think you believed it. Shit like this blows over if you give it some time."

She shoves her books to the floor and gets up. "You don't *get* it. They aren't some little rumors. You're a complete joke around the school, do you realize that? All my friends are talking about it."

"All your friends are morons who need better hobbies if entertainment to them is listening to stupid rumors." I stare at my history book, but the words have blurred together and I have no idea what I'm reading. "Leave it alone."

Jasmine folds her arms stiffly across her chest and huffs out a sigh. She's still and silent but I can feel her eyes boring into me, so I look up and stare right back. It doesn't take me long to figure out what she's thinking, the ultimate question on the tip of her tongue. "You want to know if it's all true? You actually want to ask me that?"

She shifts her weight from one foot to the other. "I didn't say that."

"But you were thinking it." My eyes narrow. "Do you honestly, sincerely think I've slept with those guys?"

"No," Jazz says. "I think you slept with Wade and it pissed someone off and the rumors got out of control."

I'm developing a tick in my left eye from all of this crap. "I haven't slept with Wade."

"Uh huh."

"I *haven't*. Unlike you, I don't make it a habit of lying to my family."

"Bull shit you don't. You wouldn't even tell the truth about you two dating!" Jazz begins to pace the short length of our room.

I draw in a slow, even breath. "No, I'm not. He wasn't—and isn't—my boyfriend. People made assumptions and I just never corrected them. Why would you believe everyone else over your own sister?"

She whips around to glare at me. "Why should I believe you? You've been acting totally bizarre lately and you've been hanging out with him all the time. I see the way you look at each other. Don't try to tell me there's nothing there."

My bewilderment rapidly morphs into amusement. I can't help but start laughing. The fact that I'm arguing with Jasmine about whether or not her very gay sister likes a very gay guy is too hilarious.

Jazz scrunches her face into an offended scowl. "What's so funny?"

"*You.* You're funny." I spread my arms wide and shake my head. It's funny, yes, but my feelings are hurt all the same and the entire situation is starting to infuriate me. "But you know what? It's cool. Think what you want. Don't believe me even though I'm your sister. Whatever."

She bristles, shoulders lifting with tension. "Because you're *lying*!"

I flip the book off my lap and swing to my feet in one fluid movement, startling Jasmine into taking a quick step back. "I'm not lying, Jasmine! I'm *gay.*"

The room goes quiet. Jasmine stares at me with eyes as wide as plates and her mouth slightly agape. "Huh?"

I don't know why I let myself blurt it out. I should have more self-control than that and yet, for as fast as my heart is racing in anticipation of what the next few seconds are going to mean for me and my sister, I'm *relieved.* Just to finally spit it out for someone to hear makes me feel as though a weight has been lifted off my chest. Since my big secret is out there in the open, I might as well fill her in to wipe that stupid look off her face.

"Gay," I repeat. "You heard me. I like girls, Jazz. I don't like guys. Wade is most definitely a guy. Therefore I am not interested in Wade. Are we clear on that?"

She closes her mouth, opens it again, and shrinks back a bit. "Yeah."

I take a deep breath and pull away, the relief starting to fade as the panic settles in. “Fantastic. Now if you’ll excuse me, I have homework to do and a play to study for.”

With that, I take a seat again and pick up my book. Jasmine is silent, seemingly absorbing what I’ve laid on her, but she doesn’t ask questions. Doesn’t try to talk about it. After a few minutes of watching me like I’ve grown two heads, she leaves.

I don’t worry about her telling anyone. She won’t want her friends to know, and after everything I’ve kept from our parents over the years for her sake, I would like to think she wouldn’t be cruel enough to tell Mom.

Or maybe I don’t care enough anymore to bother.

Diary of a Noble

There is something to be said for keeping secrets. Ignorance is bliss. You can't worry about things like death if you aren't raised to know what death is, right? To think you could live forever would be the ultimate bliss...but also the biggest lie for someone to believe.

When my sister was six, I had to explain to her why her pet hamster wouldn't wake up. I couldn't do it. Instead, I boxed the hamster up and buried it without telling her, then swore the hamster must have escaped. For years, she lived in the ignorant bliss of assuming her beloved pet was off frolicking in a hamster paradise somewhere.

The more I think about it, the more I come to the conclusion that I have never wanted anything more than for J to be safe and happy and shielded from everything that made me sad growing up. When Mom and Dad fought, I would take her into the bedroom and we'd put my headphones on and listen to music at top volume. When Dad spiraled deeper into his addiction and I did not understand what was happening, I made up stories for him to explain away his behavior: "Daddy is sleeping right now, he's not feeling well."

Then we grew apart and I stopped being able to shield her from things. The harshness of social life, Dad's issues, the fact that Mom is not Wonder Woman and can't always be there when we need her and, sometimes, we have to be there for each other. We're sisters. That's what we do.

Now that I've had a few hours to dwell on what I told J last night, I think the one thing I wanted to hear her say more than anything else in all the world was: "It's okay, I still love you."

22

Jazz is gone in the morning before I'm even awake, meaning she undoubtedly slept in the living room and took off early to go God knows where. I will not let this affect me, I tell myself, because nothing is going to change the fact that I told Jasmine my secret and things are never going to be the same between us.

I haven't convinced myself to get out of bed when Amber messages to ask if I want to go grab a movie and a bite to eat. I would jump at the chance...except I'm broke, and I can't justify asking Mom for money while I know she's working her butt off today. I also don't want to turn Amber down.

Maybe movie + dinner here? I can cook.

Three minutes later she writes back: *My treat.*

I groan, rolling over. *I can't let you do that*, I reply.

Someone knocks on the front door. I contemplate shoving my head under the pillow and going back to sleep, at least until Amber agrees to hanging out here. But it's nearly ten a.m. and for all I know, it could be Mom having forgotten her keys or the mail lady with a package. I haul butt out of bed and shuffle through the apartment to open the door.

Amber tucks her phone into her pocket. "Too bad."

The corner of my mouth twitches. I'm standing there in a pair of flimsy night shorts and a tank top, the cold air is making me shiver, and I'm suddenly very grateful I shaved my legs. Because Amber would totally care about that, yeah. I step aside to let her in. "I don't need you to pay for me."

"I'm aware. Are you going to get dressed or are you going out like that?"

Sighing, I let her usher me back to my room, now grateful for my sister's absence. I sit on my bed while Amber begins to pick through my closet. Her hair is tied up again, but instead of a ponytail, it's clipped up in a way that is purposefully messy. I'm so busy staring at the way the loose tendrils fall against her shoulders and around her face that I don't realize when she's standing in front of me, arm outstretched, that she's picked out clothes for me to wear.

"Hello, Earth to London?"

"Sorry." I blink, slowly reaching for the garments. "You're choosing my clothes now?"

"Well, you weren't doing it."

I study the outfit she picked out, decide it's something I would have chosen on my own anyway, and stand up to get undressed. I think about asking her to turn around like I did with Wade because there's something more intimate about having Amber see me naked, but I don't know how to say it without making it sound strange. Girls get changed around each other all the time. Up until senior year, I had to do it in front of a locker room of other people every day for gym. How is this different?

Because it's Amber, is the only differing factor.

I shimmy out of my shorts and pull off the tank top. Amber is busying herself looking down at her phone, thankfully. Gives me time to slip into fresh clothes before she's paying attention to me again. There isn't much else I do to get ready aside from ducking into the bathroom to wash up, brush my teeth, and try to make some sense of my hair. I'm not a huge makeup person beyond a tube of lip gloss.

Amber is waiting patiently for me when I emerge. I am not a morning person—never mind it's hardly morning anymore; I just woke up which means it's morning to me—and therefore it hasn't even occurred to me to ask where we're going. Amber is quiet, so I slouch down in the front seat of her car with a yawn, and let het take me wherever she's taking me and listen to the light rainfall against the windshield.

Our destination is the mall downtown. Or rather, the theater attached to the mall. While I have zero problems with us going to a movie and hanging out, her method of planning this is bizarre.

Showing up at my house like she did and insisting on dragging me out of bed instead of the casual plan-making we're prone to doing. Add that to the fact she's being quieter than usual and has an almost determined look on her face...I'm really not sure what's going on. I don't question it just yet. I peer up at the scrolling marquee while Amber purchases our tickets.

"Two for *Passing for Dead,* please."

My gaze returns to her, surprised. It's a movie I mentioned weeks ago that I wanted to see and she hadn't seemed terribly interested. Amber returns to me, offering a ticket, and I take it with a lopsided grin. "You remembered."

She shrugs. "It was the only thing playing."

Nevermind that I can see that's a lie. I playfully link one of my arms with hers before she can get far, and we head into the theater arm-in-arm.

Passing for Dead is everything I had hoped it would be: pointless horror and gore with enough frightening imagery to give me nightmares for weeks. Perfection. Amber turns to me when we step out of the theater, and I'm still going on about the special effects of the main character's love interest being turned—quite literally—inside out by the zombies. I become aware she's waiting for me to stop talking, so I do, and she asks, "If you could pick anywhere you want to eat for lunch, where would it be?"

That catches me off guard. Despite having eaten popcorn during the movie, I'm starving again. The logical assumption would be that we'd grab our lunch from someplace cheap within the mall. "There's a pizza place at the food court that isn't half bad."

She shakes her head. "That's not what I asked. If you could pick anywhere."

I study her, trying to figure out what could possibly be going through her head. "Are you all right today?"

Amber rolls her eyes. "Can you answer the question?"

"Okay, okay." I run a list of places through my head. Really, I don't eat out all that often, so I couldn't tell her what my favorite restaurant is. When was the last time I ate at a sit-down place, anyway? Oh. Right. My "double-date" with Mara, Trevor, and Wade. While I could suggest Bruno's and Mom isn't working there today, I'm not sure I want to risk anyone who knows me there saying anything to us.

"There's this diner called Rosie's Kitchen a few blocks away," I offer tentatively. I'm not used to someone paying for me. Are there rules for this kind of thing? Like, is something cheap considered an insult? Is something expensive too forward? I wasn't thinking about it with Wade because he covered my check without giving me a choice.

Amber seems to relax. "Okay. Rosie's Kitchen it is."

It's close enough to walk but the rain is coming down in sheets when we emerge from the mall, so we end up driving anyway. Rosie's is relatively empty. There are a few Halloween and fall decorations lining the counter tops and orange lights framing the menu. We choose a place near the windows, a few booths over from where I sat on my double date.

After we've placed our orders, Amber slouches back in her seat and stares out the window. It's the first time we've had a real moment of silence since she dragged me out of the house. First there was the movie, and then she had the radio up in the car on the way here. Now there is just the soft patter of rain outside, and the silence between us.

"So," I venture, "are you going to tell me what's going on?"

Amber doesn't look at me. "What do you mean?"

"You haul me out of bed and march me to the theaters and then out to eat with no warning. All pushy-like. What gives?" It's hard to pinpoint what about it is strange, other than it's not very Amber-like. She's so mellow about making plans.

"I don't know." She squirms in her chair, lifts a hand to mess with a strand of her hair, only to realize it's clipped up. Her hand drops uselessly to her lap. "I wasn't sure if you'd want to go out with me."

Go out with me. She says it like this is some sort of date.

Which...it kind of is. A movie and a meal, and she's insisting on paying for everything. Now that I'm looking closer, it dawns on me she's wearing a blouse and a skirt that hangs to just above her knees. I have never seen Amber in a skirt. Not to mention she's actually put in her contacts and is wearing jewelry.

The ensemble isn't fancy, exactly, but it's something I would normally reserve for, like, holidays or a birthday.

I can feel my ears growing hot. No, no. I'm totally overthinking this. Amber and I are not on a date. We are not involved that way. She doesn't even know I play for that team, or that I really like the way she twists her hair around her fingers. Or the way her glasses slip down her nose when she's hunched over a set with a paint brush in her hand, tongue between her teeth. She has no clue I kind of like the shape of her mouth like her bottom lip is made for me to run my thumb over it.

I used to admire little details like this about Mara, once upon a time. Now I can't recall the last time I looked at her and thought anything of the sort. Mara is still sweet, lovely Mara, but getting to know her seems to have taken away some of the magic.

Then there is Amber. She was this nonentity sitting in the back of the theater when I first walked in. Mouth downturned, hair pulled back, baggy clothes, uninvolved with everything around her. She blended. I did not notice. Somewhere along the line, that changed.

"London?" she asks, eyeing me. "Your face has gone all funny."

"Has it?" God, I have to get my head on straight. (Hahaha...ha.) I run a hand through my hair, glancing toward the kitchen and anxious for our food to arrive so I have something to shove into my mouth to avoid having to speak.

Amber plucks a napkin from the holder and begins tearing it into pieces. In half, then in quarters, in sixths. "I guess I'm sorry for being pushy. I shouldn't have forced you." Eighths. Tenths.

My spine straightens. "What? No, no. That's not what I meant. You didn't *force* me. It was actually a nice surprise getting taken out and treated to this. No one has ever done that for me before." Well, Wade paid for my double-date, but it didn't feel the same.

She stops tearing, instead rolling a shred of napkin into a little ball between her fingers. "Really?"

"Really."

"That's stupid." A frown tugs at her face. "Everyone does at least once in awhile."

I'm itching to ask her if this is a date. If it could be. Amber is so nonjudgmental and laid back, maybe...

I say, "Then next time it'll be my treat." Not that I have a clue where I'll get the money, but I'll figure something out.

The frown eases off of Amber's brow and is replaced by the ghost of a smile. Her shoulders relax. She abandons the napkin. "Okay."

Our waitress brings us our food. We dig in, finish half our plates, then swap to try each other's meals. The egg rolls she ordered are heaven and she makes a pleased noise at the taste of my French dip sandwich.

I'm still chewing when my phone goes off. Jazz's ringtone. After last night, I don't know what she could possibly think she would want from me. Maybe she locked herself out of the apartment or something. Regardless, I ignore it. I'm eating. I'm enjoying myself. I'll drop her a text when we leave here.

Except the phone rings again.

Amber arches an eyebrow. "Going to get that?"

I swallow my food as I dig the phone from my pocket and bring it to my ear. "What?"

Jasmine's words spill out like she's been holding her breath, waiting to get it out. "Can you pick me up?"

There's a desperate edge to her voice that stops me from asking why the hell she can't take the bus home. "Where are you? What's wrong?" I lean back and abandon my fork. Amber looks up, curious.

"Dad's. We sort of..." Jazz flounders, sniffs, tries again. "Can you just come get me? Please?"

Every worst case scenario runs through my head.

"I'll be there as soon as I can," is what I promise before hanging up.

Amber wipes her mouth on a napkin, already rising from her seat. "Where are we going?"

"I'm sorry," I'm quick to say. "I need to get home and then go pick up my sister from my dad's. She sounded really upset."

She tosses me her keys and picks up the check from the end of the table. "I can take you, if you want." Then she's heading up front to pay for our meal, leaving me to mull over what she said as I duck out into the rain and head for her car.

It's true, Dad's house is just a few blocks from here and would take a lot less time to grab Jazz now rather than have to go home myself to get my car and then return to this part of town. But then again...this requires a great deal of opening myself up. Letting Amber potentially see and hear something about my life I'm not sure I want her to see or hear. What if Dad causes problems? What if Jazz is a hysterical mess?

I buckle in and start up the car to let the heat begin defrosting the windows. Amber joins me a minute later. "So...where to?"

She means *am I taking you home or are we doing this?* I bite at the inside of my cheek and look at her. Were it anyone else...maybe I'd say no. I'd ask them to take me home. But I'm worried about Jazz, and...

I trust Amber. More than anyone else outside of my family, I trust her.

So I say, "Head up to Wilson Avenue and take a left."

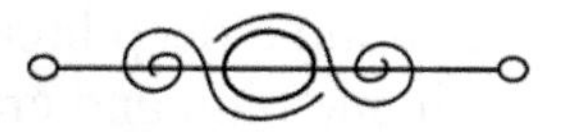

The rain comes down in torrents. Welcome to fall in central California. Hot and dry one day, pouring the next. I tell Amber she doesn't have to come up—I'd almost rather she didn't—but as I'm heading for the stairs, I hear her car door open and close and the sound of her steps not far behind me.

I'd hoped Jazz would be waiting outside. She isn't. Upstairs we go and I don't bother knocking. His door is unlocked, so I shove it open and step inside, fear and anger bubbling inside me like an oncoming storm.

"Jasmine? Hello?"

Jazz rises from the couch the moment she hears me, holding a finger to her lips. "He's sleeping."

"I don't give a fuck if he's curing the common cold. What happened?" All it takes is for me to step closer to see the sizeable cut and bruise on her temple. The little storm in my chest evolves into a five on the Richter scale.

It must register on my face, because Jazz flings herself at me to grab hold of my arm. "It wasn't him!"

I twist free, marching for the bedroom. I'm going to kill him. That's all there is to it. I'm going to make him sorry he was born. Jazz throws her arms around my waist, near hysterics.

"He didn't. London, please!" When I try to shove her off, she continues, "He yelled at me and I freaked out and slipped. I cracked my head on the counter. That's all. I swear!"

I stop a few feet from the door, chest heaving, and pulse flying at hurricane speed. One look at her panicked face and I know she isn't lying. However as far as I'm concerned, scaring her to the point that she hurt herself while trying to get away from him? Still counts. He caused this even if he didn't lift a hand against her directly. I want to bash his kneecaps in with a meat tenderizer.

"London." Amber's voice is soft but the startling contrast between that and Jasmine's sobbing draws my attention. She is watching me, patient and knowing. "Why don't we get Jasmine home?"

I look at my sister, taking a deep breath. She doesn't loosen her hold on me. "He came home high and crashed. You can't wake him up anyway."

Screaming at an unconscious parent isn't likely to make me feel any better, I'll agree. "Let's go home."

Amber carries Jasmine's backpack while I walk side by side with my sister, an arm around her shoulders. Jazz is silent the ride home save for the occasional sniffle, and Amber doesn't even try to turn the radio on. Mom is at work when we get to the apartment. Probably for the better. There's no way we can hide that half of Jasmine's forehead is black and blue, but at least this gives me a chance to talk to her first.

While I take Jazz to the bedroom, Amber lingers in living room. I get Jazz some aspirin, figuring she's got to have a splitting headache, and help her get settled into bed only after I've checked her eyes to make sure she doesn't have a concussion.

"No ringing in your ears?" I ask as I pull the blankets up around her. "No throwing up?"

She hunkers down beneath the covers, looking tiny and young. She is little fifth grade Jasmine who needed me to take care of her when she had pneumonia. "No, I'm okay."

I run a hand over her hair gingerly, offering an apologetic smile. "We're going to have to tell Mom, you know. She's going to flip, but I'll talk to her. Try to spare you most of it."

Jazz sighs. "Yeah. I know."

"She's not going to want you to visit him anymore."

"I don't want to." She sounds so small and guilty when she says it. "I don't want to see him again. He scared me. He was just so... How am I supposed to help him when he's like that?"

It's music to my ears. Maybe later, she'll change her mind, but it's the first time Jazz has ever said such a thing and I want to believe it. I rub her arm through the blanket. "You can't. No one can help him until he wants it—*really* wants it—for himself. You did everything you could. Don't let him or anyone else tell you otherwise."

She seems to mull this over. "...Why did you come get me?"

I push my shoulders back, eyebrow raised. "You asked. Why wouldn't I?"

"After how I reacted last night. Why bother?"

How do I tell her it didn't even cross my mind? That our previous conversation was a complete nonissue? "Because we're sisters, and that's what sisters do. I promise you, Jasmine, there will never be *any*one in your life that has your back like I do. Got it?"

Jasmine's lashes lower; she nods and I leave her alone in the dark room with Pooky, a stuffed bear she's had since she was five and normally keeps in her closet. Now she's clutching it to her chest like it's going to keep her head above water.

Before I can leave Jasmine asks, "About Amber..."

I pause, hand on the doorframe. "What about her?"

"Is she, like, I mean..." Her thin brows knit together. "If you and Wade weren't really dating, then are you and her together or something?"

A few butterflies work their way up through my stomach. "No, she's just a good friend."

"Oh. But do you like her?"

"Do I *act* like I like her?" I'm genuinely curious about this.

"I think so." My sister shrugs, curling a strand of her hair around her finger and studying it. This must be weird for her to talk about, but she's making an effort and I appreciate that. "I don't think I've ever seen you look at someone the way you look at her."

I try not to smile as I feel my cheeks and the tips of my ears growing hot. "What way is that?"

Jazz rolls her eyes. "Like...I don't know. When you were looking at her in the car, there was this weird expression on your face."

I have to laugh. "I'll keep that in mind so I'm not too obvious."

"Maybe you should be obvious," Jazz offers, and then rolls over with Pooky still in her arms, ending the conversation.

Be obvious, huh? What a quick path to rejection.

Amber is still waiting in the living room, seated on the couch and flipping through a TV Guide.

"I'm really sorry." I take a seat beside her. She closes the booklet, sets it aside, and draws one of my hands in both of hers, smoothing her thumb over the crescent grooves I've cut into my palms from fisting my hands so tightly the entire trip home. They sting.

She says, "I don't know why you're apologizing to me."

"Because this kind of ruined our little date." I don't think I should be using that word. *Date.* Too obvious, yeah, and I'm not taking advice from Jazz. But it's there and Amber only gives me a soft look and doesn't correct me. Of course she wouldn't. Not at a time like this.

"Things happen. I'm sorry I couldn't help more."

"You did help. You helped a lot. Sometimes...it's nice just to have someone there, you know? Makes me feel less alone."

Amber nods, but she says nothing. She doesn't honestly need to. Everything is said by the fact she stuck right by my side, and that she's sitting here, tightly holding my hand.

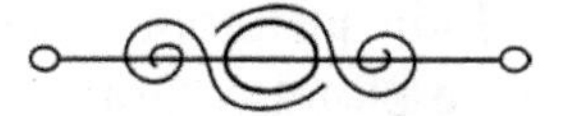

By the time Mom is off work, Amber has gone home for the night. Jazz emerged from her room long enough to nibble at some dinner I put together, and has since retreated to sleep. I've waited up because the longer I wait to talk to Mom, the harder it's going to be and the more tempted my sister and I will be to keep it to ourselves.

When Mom shuffles in the door and sees me still awake, bundled up in a blanket on the couch in the dark with late night television on low, she's instantly worried. I don't know how to alleviate that any, even when I say, "No big deal. Get settled and all that first."

Of course, it *is* a big deal. It's a major deal. After I've explained everything, Mom sits on the other end of the couch, teary-eyed and devastated and infuriated all at once. I can't recall ever seeing her so angry. Her jaw is tight, her shoulders square and tense. Normally, upset Mom looks small and sad. But upset and pissed off Mom looks ready to tear out the throat of anything that threatens her family.

I try to reassure her it's okay, that Jazz has said she isn't going back to Dad's, that he can't force us to. Yeah, he has joint custody, but I'm eighteen now and all it would take is a statement from Jasmine to say she wants nothing to do with him and CPS searching his apartment and seeing how he's living to keep her from that ever again. That's the nice thing about being older. We have a lot more of a say in what happens to us.

Eventually Mom pulls me to her and kisses my forehead, half-heartedly scolds me for not calling her at work, but thanks me for taking care of my little sister, all in the same breath. Worn out, I get up to head to bed and Mom stops me with a quiet, "I'm sorry, London."

I stop just shy of the hall, frowning. "For what?"

Mom rubs her hands over her denim-clad thighs, breathing in deep. "You're always left with these things. These...big things that *I* should be taking care of. It isn't fair."

"I don't mind," I say, and I mean it. "You're busy. Dad is useless. There's no reason I can't try to help out."

"You're a kid." Mom has stopped crying by now, but her eyes are red and puffy, face blotchy. Gotta say, none of the girls in my family are pretty criers. Me included. "It's not your job. You should be...doing stuff. Having fun. Going to parties. Sneaking out or whatever it is kids do these days."

I smile faintly. "You're the only mother in existence that would lecture me about *not* doing things I shouldn't."

"It would remind me I haven't completely robbed you of a normal childhood." She tries to smile back.

"I promise, Mom. You haven't robbed me of anything." Maybe my life isn't quite what the lives of other kids I go to school with, but who cares? My life has made me who I am, and for the most part, I'm good with that.

"You can't look me in the eye and tell me that's true." Mom rubs at her eyes, which does nothing for the redness. "You don't go to parties or sleepovers. You've never had a boyfriend. You don't go to dances. All the things—"

"That Jazz does?" I snort. "I don't have to do those things to be happy. I *have* friends." Sort of. It's complicated. "Anyone who needs a boyfriend to be happy is lacking something in their life."

Mom looks at me again. Really, really looks at me. "What about Wade?"

I try not to laugh. "Wade isn't interested."

That gets her to frown. "Well, why not?"

She sounds so affronted that a boy wouldn't like one of her daughters. It's cute. "Because he's just not, Mom. I don't know. It isn't like that with us. Wade isn't much for dating."

Thankfully, Mom isn't much in the mood for questioning further. She looks tired and weighed down. She gives me a soft smile and says, "Someday, you'll meet someone who will be perfect for you."

It takes everything I have to smile back at her. “I know it. Good night, Mom.”

23

Monday means I'm back in my school approved clothes: white button-up, black pants. That doesn't keep me from pulling on my black boots, a bright hair clip and some jewelry, compliments of Amber and the mall.

Jasmine ducks inside on her own, as per usual, while Amber greets me at the double doors with a small smile that I try to return.

"Just because we dealt with drama club doesn't mean I'm not still a social pariah with most of the rest of the school," I warn. "You sure you want to be seen with me?"

Amber shrugs. "I've dealt with worse things in my life than being looked at sideways because some people are idiots."

"Suit yourself."

We stroll down the halls and I'm trying to exude confidence even if the idea of approaching my locker is making me nauseous. Amber hovers close, and I know she's watching to see if she spots anything pasted to the front of it.

Not that anyone bothered with pads this time. Or notes. Of course not. Sharpie is a lot harder to get off of a locker door, which has now been adorned with *Dirty London* across the front.

Amber reaches for my arm. "Come on. We'll report it to the office and they can clean it off."

I stare at the words for a few moments. "No. Leave it."

"What? Why?"

"Because they'll just keep doing it." I open the locker to cram my things inside. "So...leave it. It's not like erasing it makes them think any differently of me."

Amber frowns. "You're a lot calmer about this than you were the other day."

I shut the door again and turn to face her with a shrug. "I don't know. Maybe things were put into perspective over the weekend. I mean, everything that happened with my sister. Priorities or something. I can still be me while ignoring all of this, can't I?"

Her grip on my arm tightens briefly and at first I think I've said something wrong. Amber isn't even looking at me, though. I follow her gaze to Missy and her friends across the hall, huddled and conversing. Which isn't unusual in of itself...but the fact that Missy looks like someone has just run over her puppy and several of them are staring in my direction makes a knot form in my stomach. Great.

"Missy is still dating Allen, isn't she?" I ask.

"Last I heard, he dumped her. Why?"

"Allen is a friend of Trevor's. He smacked my ass one day in the hall."

"Probably not good, then," Amber murmurs. The two of us continue to stare until Missy and her girlfriends look away and I take it as a small triumph. I refuse to do anything other than keep my chin up as we pass by them, even as one of them coughs "dirty slut" as we go.

No. I have to keep my eyes forward and my chin up. I won't let them win.

I head to Ms. Scheck's class with a full stomach, compliments of Amber's mother who was ever so kind to pack some extra food today which Amber shared with me. Home cooking. It beats a PB&J sandwich and an apple, I've got to say.

Mara doesn't smile when she sees me. Her lips are pursed together in that way she does when she's concerned about something. The moment I sit down, she twists in her seat to lean over. "I've been looking for you all day."

Uh oh. "Is something wrong?"

"It's Allen Hecklin. Do you know him?"

My spirits sink and the food in my belly isn't feeling so great. "Sort of. I know who he is. Why?"

"He's being added to the list," she whispers. "He's saying you and him went out last weekend."

"Gag me with a fork." I run a hand through my hair, sighing. "That would explain why Missy was staring daggers at me this morning."

"They had a rough breakup just last week. Missy isn't a bad girl. She's really not. But..."

"But it looks suspect that he dumps her and then he's supposedly out with me. I get it." As stupid as it may be. "What should I do?"

Mara frowns. "I don't really know. I've tried talking to Trevor to get him to do something. No luck there."

"Of course not. Helping would require him to admit he did something wrong in the first place." Unless we have solid proof that Trevor lied, I can't picture him admitting to anything. Even then...

Ms. Scheck clears her throat. "Mara, London? I hate to break up your conversation, but class is starting."

We sink back into our seats while I'm busy plotting Trevor's murder in my head. Or at least his total and complete humiliation in front of the whole school. If this were a dumb 90's movie, I could play the ultimate prank to do just that. Unfortunately, I'm stuck settling for moping about it all the way through class and into the hall, where Mara says she has to get a few things from her locker and then she'll join me at drama club.

I take my time going down the halls, secretly hoping I'll run into Trevor. Or Allen. Or any other of the guys whose names are emblazoned in my mind as having supposedly had a roll in the hay with me. Ricky, Grant, Brian, Roland. All but one of them on the swim team. All of them single with nothing to lose. Saying Trevor didn't have some kind of influence on that? No way.

As I round the corner and head out the double doors to cross the quad for the drama room by the cafeteria, I run right into (almost literally) Missy.

To say this is coincidence would be stretching it, and yet by the surprised look on her face, I have to think it must be. I really wanted to talk to Allen and set the record straight before approaching Missy about anything, but here we are, and here she is...bringing a hand up to slap me.

The sting makes me jerk back, bringing a hand to my face. It takes a lot of self-control not to haul out and punch her out of pure reflex. "What the *hell?"*

"That's what I should be saying," Missy hisses. "How long, huh? People told me he's been hooking up with some slut in the bathrooms between classes for two months and I didn't want to believe it. But it was you, wasn't it? The whole time..."

My mouth drops open. I'm too stunned to speak. Her shouting has drawn attention and a few people wandering by have slowed to a stop to watch. Two of Missy's friends have come from the direction of the drama building and flank her, hyenas ready to attack.

I lower my hand slowly. "Look, I don't know about any of that, but I did *not* hook up with Allen. He's really not my type."

"Oh, of course you'd lie about it. Just like you lied about Trevor." She laughs. The sound drips venom. "No one wants to be known as the school skank."

My heart is trying to crawl up my throat and run away. Every inch of my being wants me to turn tail and flee but I refuse to give into it. "You've got that wrong. If I had sex with all those guys, I wouldn't have a problem admitting it. Anyone else here think that I slept with their boyfriend?"

Two girls raise their hands. The first says, "Grant."

"Grant mentioned me by name, did he?"

She hesitates. "Well, no. But..."

"So you find out your boyfriend cheated on you and because of the rumors going around, you assumed it was me. Is that right?"

The girl scuffs her shoe against the concrete and averts her eyes. The second girl pushes to the front of the growing crowd. "My best friend's boyfriend got caught last month with a girl behind the school. Nobody knew who it was, but the description matches you perfectly. Platinum blonde hair and everything."

This is fucking hysterical. "Last month, huh?"

"That's what I said."

"Considering I didn't bleach my hair out until last week, I wonder how that works."

She pauses, mouth opening and closing while I scoop the wind right out of her sails. I turn to Missy, arms spread. "Think about it. None of you even knew my name before this year. Why would I all of a sudden decide to go around sleeping with every one's boyfriends?"

"You tell me," Missy growls, but there is doubt in her voice this time, like she's asking herself the same question.

I'm so done with this conversation. Too many people are watching. Nothing I say will get through to any of them. So I simply start to walk past her.

I don't realize Missy is swinging at me until it's almost too late. Her fist grazes my jaw as I jerk back. She doesn't waste any time grabbing my hair. I swipe at her face, awkward with how she's wrenching my head to one side. When that doesn't work, I grab a fistful of her hair—and a hoop earring along with it—and yank. Hard.

Missy lets out a shrill howl and all I can think is *I hope I ripped her earring out* followed by *Oh holy shit please tell me I didn't rip her earring out.* That noise she makes is all it takes to bring out the other wolves. Her friends are on me. I hit the ground, the back of my skull smacking the concrete hard enough to make me see stars. Someone hits me in the face and I taste blood in my mouth. A foot connects with my side. Once. Then again. Then multiple boots and sneakers are driving into me and it's all I can do to curl in on myself and wrap my arms around my head to prevent my face from getting kicked in.

"Get the hell away from my sister!"

Jasmine's voice is a light through the fog. When the assault stops and I'm finally able to look up, I see her standing there. Not just her, either, but three of her friends poised nervously but steadfastly at her back, displaying no intention of running away from the older girls. From the opposite side of the crowd, Mara and Amber push through and come to me, hands under my arms to help me to my feet. I'm dizzy and I hurt, but nothing is broken aside from my pride.

“What do you want?” Missy snarls.

Jasmine matches her furious look tenfold and is in her face without a fear in the world. “Let’s start with how London wouldn’t touch anything you touched with a ten foot pole, and continue with the fact that if you *ever* lay a hand on my sister again, I’ll rip your fucking throat out.”

I stare at Jasmine, stunned. The girl who wanted nothing more than to fit in and be liked, the girl who wouldn’t even admit to having a sister...is defending me. In front of a large group of people. To girls several grades above her. Would it ruin the moment if I went up and hugged her?

A muscle in Missy’s jaw ticks. She really ought to have that looked at. “Maybe dirty skank runs in the family.” Her friends snicker, but the sound is more like the nervous whickering of horses now that the numbers have evened. “You’re telling me all the guys have lied?”

“That’s exactly what I’m saying,” Jasmine says.

Out of all the guys I’ve supposedly screwed in the last few months, only Trevor and Allen are in the crowd. All eyes turn to them, awaiting confirmation. Allen shifts awkwardly. Trevor lifts his hands up.

“The truth, Trevor,” Amber says. She’s still holding onto my arm, body positioned in a protective stance against mine while Mara flanks my other side. “I suggest you really, really think about the words that come out of your mouth.”

A flicker of mild surprise crossed Trevor’s face at Amber’s acidity and for a moment...just a moment...I think he’s actually considering telling the truth. But then he smiles easily and holds out his hands in a helpless gesture. “Why would I lie about it? It’s true.”

Everyone might believe him, I realize. No matter how this turns out, Trevor will always come out on top because people know him, people like him, and I’m a nobody. A nonentity.

My stomach lurches and my insides twist. I can’t do this anymore. These girls who are hurt, who think they weren’t good enough for their boyfriends... Girls who were cheated on, even if the offending female wasn't me... Amber being sneered at for her association to me... Wade and Mara not knowing who to believe...

"I know it's a lie," I announce, "because I haven't slept with any guy. Period. I'm gay."

All eyes turn to me. The quad has grown eerily silent. Amber's hands on my arm tighten and I feel Mara looking at me, eyes wide.

"But... You and Wade?" she whispers

"Wade was covering for me." I manage the lie easily with a shrug. "He found out and he was a nice enough guy to help me out."

"...Because she was helping me out," Wade murmurs from behind us. I don't know when he got there, but now that I feel his presence at my back I don't know how I could have missed it. "We both are. We're both—we were covering for each other."

Trevor stares at his best friend as the horror registers on his face. "Are you kidding me? Dude, you've slept at my house. You watch the whole team get changed—"

"What makes you think any of you are even remotely appealing to me?" Wade says dryly. "You're not my type. Trust me."

Missy's eyes haven't left me. In this moment, it doesn't matter that she hurt me. All I see in her expression is a wounded girl who doesn't understand what's happening, why the guy she loved would do this to her. The fact she isn't saying a word to him and looks humiliated makes me wonder if she's blaming herself.

Without a word, the crowd begins to disperse. Missy whirls around and stalks away. Her friends linger a moment longer before following. Trevor and Allen make themselves immediately scarce, slinking toward the parking lot with their metaphorical tails between their legs. The few bystanders also wander away, whispering to themselves. Whether it's about me, or Trevor, or whatever...I don't care anymore.

All that remains are me and my friends and Jasmine and hers. Jazz looks to me and the earlier anger is gone. She doesn't yell at me for spilling my secret. She doesn't yell at me for embarrassing her, for ruining her carefully constructed image. The vision of her begins to blur as the tears fill my eyes and my sister is there, wrapping her arms around me in a tight hug while she murmurs, “It’s okay, London.”

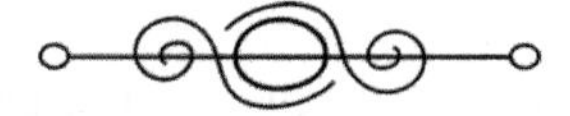

Amber follows us home. Jasmine disappears into the kitchen to make us something to eat while Amber takes me into the bathroom and sits me on the closed toilet lid. Other than my tumbles with Jasmine, I've never been in an actual fist-fight before. It took more out of me than I would have suspected a fight could. My knees are skinned and my head hurts from where it hit the ground.

Amber takes up a wash cloth from the counter and runs it under cold water and then turns to dab at the corner of my mouth. The initial contact doesn't sting like I expect it to. In fact, the cold feels nice. The only part that doesn't feel so great is her trying to wipe up the drying blood dribbling down my chin.

When she pulls away to rinse the wash cloth I ask, "Did I win?" and Amber turns to raise her eyebrows at me before shoving the rag against my face. This time it stings a little. Ow.

"Hm. I wonder." Her shoulders lift and fall in a sigh. "Let's not make this a habit though, okay?”

“I tried to leave it alone. I didn’t mean for it to escalate like it did. I didn’t mean to tell everyone...” The thought makes me tear up and I try not to let them escape because I know it will sting my cuts. I squeeze my eyes shut instead.

"There's no reason for crying," Amber murmurs, but it isn't a chastising statement. Her fingers touch my cheek. "Everything is going to be okay."

Sharing such close space with Amber right then and there, I think that I’m not afraid anymore. Amber knows and she’s still here. She’s still with me. Mara and Wade kept at my heels walking to the car and Mara fussed over me worriedly the whole way. They know and they still care. Amber has accepted every little quirk and crisis of mine with barely more than a roll of her eyes.

I ask, “It doesn’t bother you? That I’m gay?”

Amber doesn't flinch. She doesn't pull back. She meets my gaze as steady as ever, and I wish she were easier to read because her eyes are so pretty but I have no idea what that look on her face means. She presses the wet towel to my split lip. "I kind of thought you were before you said anything."

My fingers clutch at the edge of the counter. "You did?"

"Sort of." She shrugs, disconnecting from eye contact in order to pry my left hand from the counter and examine the scrapes on my knuckles. "I mean, obviously I wasn't sure enough to ask, but I had a feeling."

"And it doesn't bother you?"

"Why would it bother me?" Amber glances up. If I didn't know better, I would say her cheeks are a little bit pink. "I like you for who you are, London. You're smart and you're unique. You've got this loyalty to your family that I really admire. And..."

"And?"

"You got me to stop being afraid. I was content to ride out the rest of high school with my head down, feeling like what happened with Trevor was my fault. I finally feel like I won that battle, and it's thanks to you."

I have to smile, wringing the wash cloth between my hands. "That was all you, girl. I didn't do a thing."

"It was both of us, then." She shrugs.

"Our powers combined sort of thing?"

"Maybe so."

Her fingers brush my cheek again on the spot where Missy first hit me. Her touch is gentle and warm. I can't help it. I lean into her hand and close my eyes like I'm starved for human affection. I'm so focused on the simple bliss of it that it takes me a minute to comprehend what she's leaning in to do.

She kisses me.

My mind blanks and I'm immediately reacting, immediately kissing her back. I am not worrying about how I'm kissing or why or anything. All there is in my world right now is Amber and how her mouth feels like home, how I don't care that her hands cupping my face are stinging my cuts because this? Totally worth it.

I pull back first but it takes effort to do so. Amber smiles a little. "Was that okay?"

My brain is still lost in the fog somewhere. "Yeah. No. I mean—that was *more* than okay, but I'm..."

"A girl? I figured that out." She lowers her lashes, taking the wash cloth from my hands and turning to rinse it in the sink. "I don't mind if you don't mind."

Here is a woman that never ceases to amaze me. It's kind of funny, really. Not that long ago I was lamenting the fact Mara would never look twice at me. Now, I can't imagine this being us. I can't imagine her being here in Amber's place. My feelings for Mara seem like a distant memory and it's hard to remember a time wherein I didn't look at Amber and feel my pulse flutter.

I stand, ignoring the ache in my skinned knees. It's a bold move but it seems right, feels right, just to step up behind Amber and turn her around so that I can lean in and kiss her first this time. Maybe a little clumsy, maybe a little overeager, but she reacts so quickly and so effortlessly that I congratulate myself on making the right decision. She kisses me hard, her hands in my hair, my hands against her back, like we're afraid the world is going to pull us apart.

My face hurts. My hands hurt. My ego hurts. But for the first time in ages, my heart is full to bursting.

Amber doesn't stay. She seems to think I need some time alone with my sister, and while I'm not sure why she thinks that...after she's gone, I'm kind of inclined to agree. Jasmine brings me an ice pack for my face and we sit on the couch, silent, while I nurse my wounds. They aren't *that* bad, but they're noticeable and Mom is going to have questions. Jasmine puts on the comedy channel. Neither of us is really laughing so all the jokes seem to fall flat.

I finally have the nerve to ask, "Why did you help me?"

Jazz wrinkles her nose. "What kind of question is that?"

"A legitimate one. Now everyone is going to associate the two of us together."

"Yeah, well." She takes a deep breath and looks over at me. "We're sisters. No one is ever going to have your back the way I do."

The warmth that makes me feel is indescribable. It fills me up and pushes my mouth into a smile. The next thing I know, I'm throwing myself at my baby sister, dragging her into a tight hug. She squawks and squirms but there is no malice or irritation in it. "Ew, let me go!"

I do, but only because someone is knocking at the door.

I have no idea who would be here this time of night, and by the look on Jazz's face, she doesn't either. It could be Amber, I guess, having forgotten something. My mistake is not looking through the peep hole before opening the door.

Dad stands there with his hands in his pockets. "Hey, London."

I don't know why I don't slam the door in this face. I could. I should. I *want* to. But I'm also fighting the urge to throw myself across the threshold and shove him over the balcony railing. In this instance, I want to be like Mom. I want to be capable of being the bigger person. "What do you want?"

Once upon a time, I remember Dad wearing nice suits. Not expensive, maybe, but nice. They fit him well, and I loved picking out ties at Christmas time. The gaudier, the better. The suit he's wearing now looks familiar but it's worn and wrinkled. Like he put in a lukewarm effort to look nice. It does not go unnoticed. If his cheekbones weren't so hollow and his hair wasn't so messy, maybe—just maybe—he'd appeal to me a little more as the dad I knew and loved as a little girl.

He smiles. "I came to see you. Well, both of you." He nods at Jasmine, who I hadn't realized was hovering just behind me. Whether to protect or to be protected, I don't know. Perhaps both. "I owe you each an apology."

Jasmine says nothing, so I speak for us both. "Go home."

With that, I try to shut the door. Dad snaps his hand out to catch it and the ease in which he pushes it back open and is able to step inside startles me into taking a few steps back, instantly alert, instantly on edge that this person I don't know any more is in our space.

He exhales heavily through his nose. "All right, look. I know I've made some bad decisions, but I love you girls. I'm getting help. I'm trying my best. You have to understand that I'm sick, all right?"

My ears ring with those words. That was all we heard for years. His addiction was a disease. He couldn't help it. And maybe he *is* sick, maybe he *does* need help, but I can't let him drag the rest of us down in the process. "I don't care."

Dad's smile fades. "London, listen to me—"

"I'm not listening," I snap, stepping forward regardless of how much bigger he is than me. Years ago I never, ever would have thought my dad would hurt me, but now I'm not so sure. I'm beyond caring. "Not in here. If you want to talk, we'll do it outside." Away from our home, out in plain view, and away from Jasmine.

"All right." Dad frowns but he steps away, turns, and exits the apartment. Jasmine grips hold of my hand so tightly it hurts and I have to physically unwrap each of her fingers free.

"It's okay," I promise. "Just stay here. Keep the door locked, yeah?"

"No way. I want to stay with you."

"He isn't going to try anything. But just in case..." I trail off and let the silence speak for itself. Better she be in here, watching from the window with a phone ready just in case Dad starts getting belligerent, rather than her having a nervous breakdown in the eye of the storm.

I follow Dad, locking and shutting the door behind me. His car is parked just downstairs, not even in a legitimate parking space so I wonder if he actually planned to be here long enough to have a meaningful conversation. When he turns around at his car and lights up a cigarette, he studies my face with a furrowed brow. "What happened to your lip...?"

"I got into a fight. Not that it's any of your business." I cross my arms. "You should have seen the other guy."

Dad chuckles. "That's my girl."

"No," I'm quick to say. "I'm not your girl. For that matter, none of us are 'your girls' anymore."

"Yeah, you are." He shakes his head. "You and Jasmine... Even your mother. You'll always be my girls, even if you aren't talking to me."

"We. Are. *Not*." I startle us both with the sudden rise in my voice. "You lost the privilege to say anything like that about us the first day you decided popping pills was more important than your family!"

"Lower your voice, young lady." Dad catches my upper arm and holds fast. Not hurting me. At least, it wouldn't be hurting it I weren't trying to twist away. "You have no idea what it's been like for me."

"I don't care!" Lower my voice? Ha. "You haven't given two shits about us, Dad. Not in *years*. You choose yourself over us again and again. Mom would have moved heaven and hell to help you get better, and you basically showed us that *nothing* we did was good enough and we weren't important enough to try!"

The tears are taking over, smothering my words and making it difficult to think. To talk. To get out the words I've kept locked up for so long. I only now realize why he's holding onto me, and it's because I'm hitting him. Pounding my fists against his chest and pushing him back against the car and he's letting me, just gripping my arms and watching and listening.

"I *hate* you! I hate you for leaving us and I hate you for everything you put Mom and Jazz through! You don't deserve another chance and you don't deserve me to listen to a god damn thing you say and you're going to make Jazz *just like you*!"

I shove him one more time. His back thumps against the driver's side door, makes the car wobble a little, and he lets me go. Willingly. He actually unclenches his hands and lets them fall to his sides. He stares at me.

I step back. Deep breaths. Easy does it. The ground sways and tilts beneath my blurry vision and it's all I can do to sink onto the bottom steps of the staircase. My chest aches with the mumbled words, "Why weren't we worth it to you, Daddy?"

There is a time I can remember us all being happy. We had a house. We had big Christmas dinners and we decorated the tree together. Dad would lift me up to put the star on top. I remember movie days, cuddled up on the couch between Mom and Dad with a bowl of popcorn on my lap.

Memories that are good. Memories that are sad because I never realized at the time how important they would be to me later when the Dad I knew was long gone.

Slowly the shape of Dad's face comes into focus where he's crouched down in front of me. I think I tore one of the buttons off his coat, and his tie is askew. He doesn't try to touch me, and his nearness is enough to make me want to either hit him or hug him. I hate him and I love him. Mixed emotions at their best.

"Sweetheart," Dad says and this—this is the voice of the Dad I remember. "Why did you say that?"

I sniff. "Say what? I said a lot of things."

"About Jasmine being just like me."

"Because she worries about it." I wipe at my eyes and my nose, wishing I'd thought to bring along a box of tissues. I could have hit him with it. "Don't you get it? The reason we have to struggle to get her to take her medications? Because she has this addictive personality, just like you. She's scared if she becomes dependent on anything outside of herself, she won't be able to stop. She's afraid she'll turn into you."

This is something Jasmine has never told me, but I know. I remember how much she cried the first time doctors told her she had issues that could be corrected with pills, because she was still going through seeing her own father self-medicate with anything he could find. She saw what it did to our family. In retrospect, maybe that's also why she never wanted to give up on Dad. She thought he needed the same help we told her that she did. Perhaps he does but that isn't for us to decide.

Dad does dare to touch me this time, just a thumb against my cheek to wipe some of the tears away. "You and your sister are a lot stronger than me, kiddo. I can promise you that. You've got a lot of your mother in you, y'know?" I turn my face away from him, fisting my hands in the hem of my shirt. Dad sighs and rocks back on his heels, running his hands through his hair. "I need you and your sister to know that there has never been anything in this world I love more than you."

I force myself to look up and meet his eyes. "I don't believe you."

To that, Dad purses his lips and nods. He rises to his feet. "That's about what I deserve. Maybe someday, I can prove it to you."

He touches my shoulder and leans down, pressing a lingering kiss to the top of my head. Like he did a thousand times growing up when he would leave for work, before things got bad.

I love him and I hate him. That's why it's both the easiest and the hardest thing to let him go when he walks away.

Jasmine nearly jumps on me when I come back inside. I summarize as best as I can, leaving out the parts about her. She listens while staring down at her hands in her lap, picking at her nail polish. When I'm done, she swipes at her eyes.

“What do we do now?”

“We don't do anything. The ball has been in his court for years. If he wants us in his life...”

“He has to prove it,” Jazz finishes quietly. I nod. She asks, “Do you think he will?” while dropping her head to rest against my shoulder.

I wish the answer to that was an easy one. That I could tell my baby sister that, yes, of course we matter to my Dad enough for him to get better. But I don't think it works that way. He isn't an addict because he wants to be, but because he hasn't found a way out of the hole he's dug for himself. The most I can offer to Jasmine is, “We'll see.”

24

It feels too impersonal to call or text Wade after all that's happened. Thankfully I have his address in my phone so I can drive to his house, texting only to ask *you home?* When he replies that he is, I don't say anything else.

Mr. Jones answers the door. I recognize him from the picture in Wade's house. Even on a Saturday, he's in slacks and a button-up shirt, but he has a smile for me. "Hello?"

"Hi. Um, I'm London. A friend of Wade's from school?"

Thankfully he must have heard about me, because he says, "Oh, of course. Wade's out back. Come on in."

He escorts me to the back yard where Wade is swimming laps in the pool and leaves me there. I won't ask how he's swimming in this weather. Wade hasn't even noticed I'm here, so I take a seat on the edge of the pool, removing my shoes to dip my feet in. Of course they would have a heated pool.

Wade does five more full laps before he surfaces right by my legs, planting a wet hand on the concrete beside me. He puffs out a breath of air and wipes his face, peering up.

"What are you doing here?"

I swing my legs a little, making the tiniest of splashes. "I came to see my boyfriend. Is that okay?"

He snorts and lets go of the ledge, drifting back a few feet. "I think that façade is pretty shattered."

"I'd say so." I look down at my reflection in the water. "Actually, I came to say I'm sorry. And thank you."

"I didn't do anything."

"Yeah, you did. You didn't have to step in and tell everyone. You could've played it off like I had lied to you."

"Pretty shitty thing to do," Wade says, watching me with that all too familiar intensity in his eyes. "You wouldn't have been in that situation if it wasn't for me."

I shrug. "It takes two. I made the decision just as much as you did."

He looks doubtful. "Uh huh. If I had stuck up for you sooner, maybe those rumors wouldn't have gotten so out of control."

"Eh, live and learn. I'm over it. The truth is out. At least whatever insults they want to throw about me now are more likely to be true."

Wade's expression softens. "You're pretty awesome, do you know that?"

Awesome. Not a word I've heard used to describe me, nor one that I'm particularly feeling. It's a lot easier to feign confidence than it is to actually *be* confident that everything will be all right. "I don't know about that."

"You are. You take everything in stride. Any time something kicks your legs out from under you, you just...bounce back, fighting harder than ever. I'd say that's pretty awesome."

I smile. "You clearly haven't seen my emotional breakdowns. Ask Amber about them sometime."

"Amber, huh? What's up with you two?"

"No idea what you're talking about."

Wade treads water closer, eyebrows raised. "Is that right. We're keeping secrets now?"

I push myself up to a crouch and offer a hand out to him, an offer to help him out of the water. "Sure. Does that mean we aren't even anymore?"

He takes my hand in his, and I think this might be the very first time I've really ever, truly, seen Wade smile.

"Now we are," he says lightly.

He yanks me into the pool.

25

Sunday is the first day Mom, Jasmine, and I sit down to have a meal together in awhile. I'm pretty sure Mom was supposed to work at the diner today and called in, which tells me this is important to her because I can't remember a time in recent years where she's ever not been there. I had to tell her what happened, of course. About Dad showing up, about our conversation, the pills, everything. She needed to know.

Over ham and cheese pita sandwiches, Mom folds her hands on the table and says, "I think we should talk."

I polish off my sandwich and glance at Jasmine, who looks like she's just lost her appetite. She nudges her plate away and hunches back in her chair, touching a hand to the bruise on her forehead. Neither of us respond, so Mom continues.

"I'm not going to ask for details on what happened. London already told me most of it, so I won't make you repeat it unless there is something you want to add. But I do have some questions and I need you to answer them as honestly as possible. Can you do that, sweetheart?"

My sister fists her hands atop her thighs. I reach out to cover one of them with my own. Her fingers uncurl, just enough to catch hold of mine and clutch them tight. "...Okay."

Mom takes a deep breath. She isn't good at this sort of thing, because it's usually been left to me to deal with this stuff. It isn't her fault, really; it's simply the hand we've been dealt. A mother who works a lot to keep food on the table, and an absent father who never contributed even when he lived with us. Mom asks, "You father was taking your medication off of you?"

"Not all of it but...yes."

"All right. Did you mean it when you said you don't want to see him anymore?"

The moment of truth. Jasmine won't lie. She has never lied before about her desire to keep in contact with Dad and I don't expect that to change now. I see the struggle across her face. The conflict. The guilt. Jasmine looks at me, meeting my eyes, and all I can do is smile for her to try to reassure her it's okay.

She finally murmurs, "I don't want to see him until he's completely sober."

Mom doesn't mean to look relieved, I know. I hope it doesn't show on my face, too. Relief that we can keep her safe now where we've struggled for so long. Mom scoots her chair around the table in order to take Jasmine's other hand in hers. Jasmine's eyes are beginning to water. Mom pulls her closer and kisses her forehead.

"It's okay," she promises. "You will always have us. No matter what."

That's it. Mom doesn't ask for details. Doesn't bash Dad or ask Jasmine to apologize or anything. Jasmine gave us an answer, and that's all there is to it. That was all we needed.

26

"Opening night," Mara sings, twirling in her custom-made dress. Her long dark hair is pinned up ever so delicately, giving her the appearance of a prim and proper wife rather than her smiling, happy self.

"This is a terrible idea," Wade grumbles. I keep my head down as Amber tucks the stray strands of my blonde hair beneath my cheap wig, because a whore in the twenties was not exactly going to have bleach-blonde hair.

"It's a great idea. You're the only one who knew all of Trevor's lines, so..." I won't point out that it's been fun spending the last two weeks seeing Wade act. He's better at it than I thought he would be. Seeing him out of his element and all... I almost wish we could've talked Amber into it. She's been content to stay behind stage, though, and I have to say she did a pretty awesome job on mine and Mara's makeup.

"Five minutes for *Selling Love,*" Mr. Cobb calls. The last group is clearing off their props and backdrops. The four of us crowd together, one last huddle before our big night.

"I think Mr. Script Writer should give us a speech," says Mara.

Wade frowns, mouth down-turning. "Like what?"

"Something inspirational," she replies. "What about you, London?"

I consider this a moment. "Well... We've all worked our asses off. We went above and beyond any of the other groups with our sets and costumes, and I think we're the ones with the most original and well-written script."

"Yeah," Amber says, "that first group's play about alcoholic clowns had a promising concept but the execution... Uh. Sucked."

"Exactly. So no matter what happens out there, I think we should all be proud of ourselves." Looking at their faces, I think they are proud. I know I am. Despite the odds, despite all the last-minute changes and everything we went through because of Trevor...here we are. Ready to walk on stage in front of a modest audience that includes our families.

Mom and Jasmine are out there. A month ago, Jazz would never have been caught dead coming to see me act. I don't know exactly what changed her mind, but I'm glad. Because when our play begins and I swoop out onto stage, I'm so terrified beneath the bright lights that I'm going to trip on my dress or lose my wig or forget my lines...but the second I see Jasmine and Mom in the front row, all that dissipates. My smile is sincere and the words come easily, flowing off my tongue as naturally as Mable herself would be able to speak them. On stage, I'm not Dirty London. I am not even London Noble. I'm Mable. I'm carefree and beautiful for my family, and that's all that matters.

We are the sole group in the entirety of the night who get a standing ovation. While I didn't actually kiss Mara, we pretty much perfected a fake stage kiss and made it convincing. By some miracle, no one forgot their lines. We were perfect. Amber's backdrops and prop suggestions were spot-on. Wade grabbed me back stage and hugged me and laughed. Actually *laughed.* I've never seen him so happy. We could not have hoped for it to go any better than it did.

Afterward, the five of us—with our parents in tow—enjoy a late meal at Bruno's. I sit between Amber and Jasmine while we all watch our parents at a nearby table, conversing and talking and laughing. Even Wade's mom and dad are joining in on it.

The day has left me exhausted. Jasmine drives home with Mom while I hop into Amber's car to head to her place—sleepover!—and we take our time getting there. After all the noise and excitement of the last few days (weeks? months?) the silence in the car is welcome.

I haven't had a sleepover since middle school, and the fact that it's with Amber is a little daunting. She carries my overnight bag inside while I follow after. Marge wasn't far behind us on the road so we're quick to retreat to Amber's room to avoid getting caught up in a long conversation with her chatty mother. In the morning, I'll welcome it. Tonight? I want to curl up under some warm blankets and get some much needed sleep.

Amber sets my bag on her bed and turns to face me, awkwardly toeing off her shoes. "So... Uh. There's a guest room, we can crash on the floor, I can bring in the air mattress, or..."

I'm busy tinkering with a music box on her desk. "Hm? Or?"

"Or we could sleep in my bed." She says it quickly, in a single rush of breath. When I look at Amber, her cheeks are red. I've seen her angry, I've seen her upset and a variety of other emotions. Embarrassed, though? Nervous? Not so much.

I blink slowly while I process this information. Sleep. In a bed. With Amber. I don't even know what exactly is going on with us. Sure, we've been acting pretty girlfriend-y, I think. Mostly quick kisses when we've had time alone, but still. It's been nice. I kind of think I've been the one too nervous to be more affectionate in public. Not because I care about anyone saying anything about me. I think I've gotten the worst of that already. But because...I don't want Amber being dragged into it.

A small, lopsided smile crosses my face. "Your bed is big enough."

Amber's body relaxes, her shoulders slumping and the ghost of a grin playing at her lips. "Okay."

We make quick work of brushing our teeth and grabbing some spare pillows from the guest room. It takes a lot for me to find the courage to get changed in Amber's room instead of running into the bathroom. Although she politely turns her attention elsewhere while I begin shedding my clothes, I can't help but feel vulnerable and exposed. Only after I've pulled my sleep shirt on and turned around do I catch her watching me, even if only briefly. She catches my gaze, blushes, and turns away to get undressed herself.

I try not to watch. Really, I do. I pull back the blankets and crawl into bed and study my fingernails, but I swear, Amber is taking her time on purpose. How could anyone not stare at someone like her? I remember the first day in drama club, how I thought she was the sort of person who blended in and I never would have noticed. Now, I'm not sure how I ever could have kept my eyes off of her.

She's curvy and soft. The dim light from the bedside lamp and the pale glow from the moon outside gives this stark, beautiful blue contrast to her skin as she pulls a t-shirt from her closet. I've hugged and held that body any chance I've gotten the last two weeks, but it doesn't feel like it's been enough. I want to hold onto her and never let go.

Amber doesn't seem to mind that I'm watching her when she turns around. If anything, she looks amused when I try to avert my gaze. When she slides into bed beside me, it's with her shirt on, but I'm still very, very much aware that when we lie down together, all that separates us is a thin layer of cotton and some underwear.

She flicks off the light and we settle down, staring at the ceiling. I want so badly to roll over to face her, to see what it's like to slide my arms around her and hold her while we sleep, but...

"London?"

I swallow hard. "Yeah?"

"Is this...okay? I mean, is this cool? I can sleep on the floor if you want. It's no big deal."

No, it is a big deal. If we were just friends, it wouldn't be. But this? This is big. Still, when I turn my head to look at Amber, when I see her frowning like that... "Why would I want you to sleep on the floor?"

"I don't know. I feel like I've been kind of initiating everything, and I'm not exactly good at this sort of thing, so..."

It dawns on me why she looks like that. Why she's nervous. Because after the last person she really liked...is it possible she's worried *I'm* not into this? Into her?

I roll onto my side to face her. "No. I mean—yes. I mean... This is good. This is great. I just...after Trevor, I guess I didn't want to, like, push or whatever? Or maybe I'm worried you'll realize..." That dating a girl is so totally not what she wants. I'm not sure how to handle that. It's one thing to lose someone you've never had. To lose someone you've barely gotten, though? It would break me to pieces. I'm not sure I even realized how afraid I was of that until now.

Amber laughs. A short, quiet sound. "We're both pretty sad, you know that?"

"I think we're both pretty nervous, actually."

"You could shut up and kiss me, then. That would be good."

That's an order I'll happily follow. For the first time, Amber and I are completely alone. I've discovered I love to kiss her, and I think even when it's no longer 'new' and 'exciting,' it'll still send a little shiver straight down my spine.

Besides that, Amber's hands are in my hair. She likes to curl her fingers in the messy strands and I love the gentle tugging of it. Her body presses and fits against mine so neatly and when she slides a leg across one of mine, I give into the urge to slide my fingers up her thigh, beneath her shirt, to her hip. Amber sighs pleasantly against my mouth, shifting beneath my touch and coaxing me to inch my hand up further.

There is, oddly enough, nothing sexual about it. Intimate, yes. Sexual...not so much. I just want to touch her. I want to trace the line of her spine and the curve of her shoulder blades, of her hips and belly. Amber is soon doing the same, mapping me out with her hands like this uncharted territory is the most remarkable thing in all the world.

That's all it is. And it's slow and easy and comfortable, full of warm kisses and soft sighs until we've begun to drift off to sleep. Amber on her back. Me tucked up against her side, head on her shoulder. I murmur, "I think you're kind of perfect."

The last thing I hear before drifting off is her replying, "I think we're kind of perfect together."

27

The world returns to normal. Well, maybe not 'normal,' but what I presume normal is going to be from now on. Normal is now that the whole school knows I'm gay but what they choose to focus on is, "Hey, London, your play was awesome."

Okay...maybe not everyone is that cool about it. At least any rumors or whispers that might be going on are now kept in their respective circles as opposed to stuck to the front of my locker. Trevor and Allen haven't said a word to any of us. If we pass them in the halls, they pretend we don't exist. Funny, considering we're doing the same to them.

Even Missy seems to have somehow stopped wanting to murder me. I don't know what's going through her head, just that she bumps into me while I'm coming out of the bathroom and she's going in and for a moment, I'm bracing myself to get hit again. Instead, she looks me over and simply says, "Hey, London," before stepping around me.

It's a little thing. However sometimes little things are all you need to know that someone has made peace with you.

Allen is not so lucky. Jasmine tells me on the drive home one day that apparently Missy kicked her ex-boyfriend in the crotch when he grabbed her arm at lunch. Yeah. That sounds like her, and I try not to laugh. Sort of.

Speaking of Jasmine...maybe the greatest change is between us. Which is good, because it's the most important change. She rides to and from school with me almost every day. She no longer avoids me in the halls. She hasn't yet brought any of her friends over to our place but, hey, baby steps. At least she's weeded out the friends who weren't really friends at all and kept hold of the ones who stuck by her when she needed them most.

Her change in behavior could be attributed to a lot of things. Could be that she's steadily taking her meds now. Or could be that whatever monster we constructed between the two of us since middle school has been brought to its knees with everything that's happened. Perhaps we realized that everyone in our lives, everyone at school, is going to come and go. Me and her? We're sisters. We're in it for life.

Mara got word she's been accepted into this awesome acting program at a college a few hours south. I'll be sad to see her go, but I'm excited for her. She positively glows when she's on stage and I know she'll go on to do amazing things.

Amber will, too. She's going to one of the universities here in town and I'm hoping to get some classes in at the community college. We want to get our education but stay close together while we do it. We've talked about maybe getting an apartment down the road. Marge offered us both part-time waitressing jobs at her restaurant for as long as we want them.

Wade has a few scholarships he's trying to choose between and I won't be surprised if he picks the school farthest from home. I want him to find himself out there in the real world. I want him to come back with his head held high, able to tell his parents who he really is.

Which is hypocritical, I guess. It's not like I've told Mom. I don't get the chance to. She breaks the ice all on her own one night before work, as she's tying on her apron and getting ready to walk out the door. "I'll be off tomorrow and Sunday. Oh, London? Why don't you see about inviting your girlfriend over? I don't think I've gotten to really meet her."

Jasmine and I exchange looks over our TV dinners, startled, telling me it wasn't her who spilled the beans. Maybe I didn't give Mom enough credit that she would find out or guess somehow. She makes this question so casually, though, that I don't even think to panic. I just grin.

"Yeah, Mom. I'd like that."

Diary of a Noble

I am a human being just as deserving of love and happiness as the next person.

I tell myself this every day, and I try to engrain it in J, too. Some days are better than others, but I think I'm learning to care less about what others think, so long as I'm happy with myself. I have my friends and family, people who accept me, who are there for me. The world at large is unimportant in the face of that.

The future is still laden with uncertainty. Will my and J's relationship remain this solid or will things begin to slip away from us again? Will Dad ever get better? Will A and I survive college and be as in love tomorrow as we are today? Will W ever find the same peace I think I've found with himself, with his family?

Such is life, though. Questions that will answer themselves in time. For now, the most important thing is that I know without a doubt that everything is going to be okay.

Acknowledgments

Every book I write and release is an adventure, and some are scarier adventures than others. *Dirty London* is one of the more nerve-wracking adventures I've taken for the simple reason that it's much different from my norm.

Nobody dies in it, for one thing. That's really weird for me.

In all seriousness, London is meant to be hope and light when compared to main characters like Archer or Vince. She has a positive outlook on life but at the same time, she's very much a typical high school girl: she thinks she has things more together than she does, and she thinks the outside world can't touch her when in reality, it is constantly trying to drag her down. I feel many parts of London reflect me in high school. I was never as optimistic or talented and outgoing as her, but I did have her sense of heaviness from constantly fearing what other people would think of me. Sadly, just like London, my perception was skewed. I always thought others would think worse of me than they did. (Bullies aside.)

Although a key theme in *Dirty London* was London and Wade's coping with their sexuality, I also really wanted Jasmine and London's relationship hold a spotlight all its own. Family relationships are so often underplayed or ignored all together in YA books, and I felt Jasmine played such an integral part in who London is and who she becomes.

In the end, I hope this is a story that makes people smile. I don't generally write feel-good things, so enjoy it while it lasts.

As always, thank you to all of my great beta readers—especially Jamie, who is a rock star every time around in helping me get those last-minute proof reads done. I self-publish with much more confidence when I know his eyes have gone over my words before I put it out there.

What's coming up next? Well...you'll have to wait and see.

Printed in the USA
CPSIA information can be obtained
at www.ICGtesting.com
LVHW020110010923
756929LV00001B/93